For the Telling

Sherryl D. Hancock

PRESS

Published by Vulpine Press in the United Kingdom in 2019

ISBN: 978-1-912701-76-6

Cover by Claire Wood

Cover photo credit: Tirzah D. Hancock

www.vulpine-press.com

Also in the *WeHo* series:

Chapter 1

Sure, she knew she was risking it all—all the time she'd put in, all the training, all the work... What was she supposed to do? Stop being gay because the Marines said so? Like it was that easy? No, they didn't understand. Men made her skin crawl—God knew she'd tried to do it with them often enough, and nothing ever worked. She'd tried being a girl, not the tomboy she always was; it felt wrong, it felt fake. It was fake—she was a tomboy. No, she was a butch lesbian—that's what she'd realized. Naturally it was a year after she'd enlisted in the Marines, after boot camp, after surviving literally hell on earth... and now she'd figured it out. What the fuck, Fate? That was all she could think. So now she was under the rule of "Don't Ask, Don't Tell." Fine, she wouldn't tell, and they better not fucking ask. She'd been raised not to lie. How many times had she had her ass beaten for lying? So many she couldn't even begin to count. But now it was her career she needed to protect. So that was what she'd do—she'd lie, she'd pretend to be something she wasn't, a straight woman. How hard could it be?

"I'm making this movie, with or without your help."

Jim Laughlin stared at Legend, his lips pursed. He knew turning her down wasn't wise, but she was really pushing her luck on this one.

"Legend, it isn't that I don't want to help," he said carefully. "It's just that the investors aren't really that excited about the project..."

"Because it's far too fucking real for them, right?" Legend shot

1

back.

"It's really raw, Leg…" Jim said, his florid face twitching. He didn't like telling Legend Azaria no—she never took it well.

"It's supposed to be raw, Jim—it's fucking real…" Legend stood, putting her sunglasses in place, covering her light hazel eyes. "Screw the investors; I'll pay for it myself."

"Legend…" Jim began, his tone placating.

Legend leaned over the table, putting her hands down in front of her, her mouth set in a hard line, her face right in front of his. "I'm making this movie, whether the religious right, the military, the fucking government or anyone else that has an issue with gays likes it or not. So the fucking investors have one fucking day—they don't want in, fine, I'll drain every fucking account I have to fund this movie, and then they can kiss my ass."

With that she turned and left the office in Studio City. Technically Jim was her manager, but she rarely, if ever, listened to him. She told him what she wanted, and he was expected to make it happen. Almost no one told Legend Azaria no; it wasn't a word she liked or handled well. She had a legendary temper and had been known to kick in doors, bust out windows, or damage any number of spaces simply because she had lost control of it.

She jumped into her 1970 Plymouth Barracuda, starting it with a deep roar and gunning the engine a couple of times, making the windows of the office building vibrate. She pulled out onto Sunset Boulevard, not noticing the stares she received from people along the street. Between the loud car, the blasting rock music—Mötley Crüe at the moment—and the woman driving, there was a definite draw.

Legend Azaria stood five feet seven inches tall, with a very slim frame. Her black hair was cut short, with crew-cut sides and the top worn longer, and usually there was enough product in it to make it stand up at an angle. Her slim face was finely boned, making her downright handsome, and usually she was completely makeup free, except for the occasional black liner when she wanted to make a real impression. Her light hazel eyes were almost always covered by sunglasses, and not for the reason people thought, that she thought she was too cool. Her tendency to completely obsesses about a project and forget to eat or sleep often left her with dark circles which she hid with the mirrored aviator shades. It saved all the annoying questions about her health.

On this particular day she was wearing what she'd consider her business attire. Snug-fitting slate-gray slacks with white pinstripes and a short-sleeved black cotton button-up shirt, and at her waist a thick black leather belt. On her feet she wore high combat-style black boots, with the legs of her slacks folded tightly so they met at the tops, four inches above her ankle. She wore a thick leather band on her wrist, and at her throat she always wore the same pendant—a gunmetal-black chain with a single black dog tag. Set on the left side of the tag were a series of 2 mm stones in the hues of the rainbow. On the back were the initials *G.T.G.* engraved in silver. Both of her arms were covered with tattoos—full sleeves. It gave her an even edgier look—not that it was the purpose of the tattoos, but they still elicited that image.

Gunning the 425-horsepower engine, she grinned at the burst of power as the car sped up. She knew she was pushing it—she knew the PD was looking to bust her at this point—but she just didn't care. She was pissed. How fucking dare they try to withhold money now. When she was making movies they wanted her to make, sure, here's money—now she wanted to make something that actually meant something to her… Oh, hell no. That's too edgy, Legend…

"It's what?" the clerk asked, not for the first time.

"Ustura," Legend said. "Ustura Azaria," she repeated, her patience at a very low point.

"Is that, like, Arab, or what?" the clerk asked snidely.

"It's Israeli," she replied, her tone low and dangerous now. "But I'm American enough to join the fucking Marines, so just fucking sign me in already."

She knew it wasn't the last time she was going to have to deal with the stupid prejudice of some dickhead from Bumfuck, Iowa, who'd never seen a brown person in their fucking lives.

The clerk completed her sign-in and sent her to the base commander. Legend did her best to reign in her temper all the way to the office. She almost had it under control when she stepped inside and saluted her commanding officer, her eyes trained on the wall behind his head.

"What's your name, son?" the officer asked, his southern accent quite clear.

Legend gritted her teeth. If she popped off at the commander on her very first day, she wasn't going to do well here.

"It's Legend, sir, Legend Azaria," she said, using the American version of her name. It would just be easier that way.

"Oh, you're a female," the commander said, clearly surprised.

Legend didn't respond, even though the phrase "No fucking shit" was on the tip of her tongue, to be followed with "Do you need to see my fucking uterus too?"

"So you're a combat videographer?" the commander asked. "I'm not sure about you going outside the wire—that's not a place for female personnel."

"I assure you, sir, I'm fully trained and can handle myself in the field."

"Not sure about that, Azaria," the commander said, pronouncing her name "As-ria."

"It's Azaria, sir," she said. "A-zair-ee-uh."

It was bad enough she couldn't use her given name, because they were too stupid to pronounce it. But she was damned if they were going to butcher her surname too.

The commander looked taken aback by the correction. "Okay…" he said, his tone indicating she was being a pain in his ass.

Better get used to it, buddy, she thought.

Two days later, Legend had all the funding for her movie. She'd been contacted by any number of other investors who'd heard about her problems getting funded. She'd been in Los Angeles for nine years, and she'd been working in Hollywood the entire time. She'd started out doing cinematography and had worked her way up to directing quickly, because she knew how things should look and she was good at getting them to do just that. In the past five years she'd made six movies, and all of them had received critical acclaim. Granted, the first three were independent films, but even so had made decent showings at the box office. The last two, however, had been block-busters, and suddenly she was "the hot new thing." It made her laugh. It made her think of some kind of "the kid is hot tonight" kind of thing. *Yeah, some kid, at the age of forty-four,* she thought wryly. Not that anyone ever guessed she was forty-four; she had youthful looks, which in some instances served her well and in others were a major detriment. Regardless, she knew what she was doing, and she just needed to show the world that.

The movie was technically in development, although she'd done most of the producer's job by selecting the story and starting work with the screenwriter. There'd already been a number of screaming fights with her, and Legend was seriously considering replacing the woman. Part of her really wanted to make this entire film using nothing but LGBT community members. Against her better judgment, she'd gone with a non-LGBT screenwriter, and she wasn't completely happy with the direction. She didn't get it, the way women talked to other women…

"You always run that fast, or just when you're pissed?" the cute blonde asked, standing above Legend as she lay on the ground, gasping for air.

"There's rarely a time when I'm not pissed," Legend replied, staring up at her.

The blonde canted her head. "That's a shame," she said, her blue eyes glittering with subdued humor.

"Why's that?" Legend couldn't help but ask.

"'Cause I'm betting with those straight white teeth, you've got a killer smile."

Legend couldn't help but smile at that.

"And I was right," the blonde said, smiling too. She extended her hand. *"Georgette Griffin."*

"Legend Azaria," she said, reaching up to shake the other woman's hand.

"Legend?" Georgette repeated. *"Your parents weren't expecting much, huh?"*

"Yeah, no pressure," Legend replied, grinning.

"Azaria?" Georgette said then, pronouncing it correctly. *Why could women get it perfect, when men fumbled like complete idiots? "What nationality is that?"*

"Israeli."

"Is Legend your actual name?"

Legend grinned again. "No, it's translated from Arabic."

"And what is it for real?" Georgette asked.

"Ustura."

"Okay, say that again slowly."

"Oo-stoo-ra."

"Ustura," Georgette repeated.

Legend smiled. "Perfect."

"I like it," Georgette said, nodding. *"Why don't you use it?"*

"Because too many idiot Marines can't pronounce it, and I have to explain how I'm still American even though my name is Israeli, and no, I'm not a friggin' terrorist…" Legend said, trailing off as she rolled her eyes.

Georgette bit her lip, grimacing comically. "No issues there, huh?"

"No, none," Legend said, grinning in spite of herself.

"What section do you work for?"

"I'm a videographer."

"So way better than what I do."

"Which is?"

"I'm an administrative clerk," Georgette said. "Join the Marines, see the world… see a damned typewriter…work in an office like any other schmuck…"

"No issues there…" Legend murmured.

Georgette laughed, nodding.

"So why are you 'always pissed'?" Georgette asked, saying "pissed" like she wasn't used to using a word like that.

Legend shrugged. "Too many men in the Marines?"

"Oh, that," Georgette said, rolling her eyes.

"Yeah, so sick of being told what us little girlies can't be doing, 'cause we might endanger our ability to procreate—'cause God knows that's the only thing we're good for, right?"

"Broodmares, yep."

"Sickening," Legend said. "Why do they let us join the Marines and put us through hell in boot camp so we can just be 'girls' here?"

"Not sure," Georgette said. "I really thought when I made it through boot camp they'd automatically respect me."

"Ha! Fooled you, huh?" Legend said, her expression reflecting her annoyance. "I practically had to file on my commanding officer to get sent out to the field with my unit."

"At least you get to go outside the wire," Georgette said, sighing. "Not sure why I learned to operate weapons I never get to use."

"Hey, I've been shot at…" Legend said, grinning.

Georgette laughed. "Show off!"

"That's me."

Making a quick decision, Legend put her Bluetooth in and made a phone call.

"Hey, Tula, do me a favor," she said, grinning as her assistant scrambled to find a pen—the girl was forever without a pen. "I need you to find me a writer in the LGBT community, preferably a woman."

"Can you do that?" Tula asked, clearly worried about something.

"Do what?" Legend asked, rolling her eyes.

"Hire someone because they're gay—isn't that, like, discrimination?"

"Are you kidding me right now?"

"Um… no?"

"Just do it, Tula," Legend said, sighing. "Let me worry about the barrage of complaints I'll get from the Writers Guild."

"Okay…" Tula said, letting her voice trail off. "Don't forget you have a meeting with BJ Sparks at two."

"Fuck!" Legend glanced at the clock on her phone; she had fifteen minutes. "I'll be there,' she said, flipping a quick U-turn and getting honked at in the process. Her middle finger went up immediately; it was LA—that's what you did.

Twenty minutes later she sat in BJ Sparks' office, waiting for him. Getting up, she moved to look at the series of platinum albums; the man was definitely prolific.

"Sorry I'm late," BJ said as he swept into the office, extending his hand to Legend.

"No problem, I was just about late," she said, grinning.

BJ smiled, his light blue-green eyes sparkling. "Too much to do, not enough time in the day."

"Damned right," Legend said, moving to sit down again.

"So what can I do for you?" BJ asked, leaning on his desk in front of Legend.

"I need to negotiate borrowing one of your people," Legend said, steepling her fingers in front of her.

"Who would that be?"

"Memphis McQueen."

"It's Memphis Lassiter now."

Legend looked back at him, her gaze level, indicating it was a moot point to her.

BJ grinned; she didn't bait as easily as he'd heard.

"What do you want her for?" he asked.

"Production, sound mixing. I understand she has quite the ear."

"For music," BJ pointed out.

"Sound, music, same difference."

BJ's lips twitched. "It's not really," he said. "So why do you want Memphis?"

"Because I want people on this picture that I know are committed to the project. I think she would be if I approached her about it."

"You haven't already approached her?" BJ asked, raising a dark auburn eyebrow.

Legend narrowed her eyes slightly. She and BJ weren't strangers; she'd worked with his wife on one of her earlier pictures. She liked him, respected him for his talent and commitment to his craft.

"No," she said, her look direct. "I know you have her in a contract—I didn't want to screw with that either for her or you."

BJ nodded, liking that Legend realized that it could be bad for Memphis if she were caught negotiating outside her contract with him.

"Well, her contract with me allows her to do other projects," he said. "Although I tend to think this would rise to a whole new level and require a lot more of her time than I had planned for originally."

Legend nodded. "Agreed."

BJ looked back at the woman sitting across from him. Allexxiss hadn't been able to say enough good stuff about Legend when they'd worked together a few years before. She'd told him what an amazing director Legend was, and how she seemed to really understand what the actors needed in order to give her what she was looking for. And no one was better at translating action to film; Legend Azaria lived up to her name when it came to cinematography.

He knew this would be a completely new arena for Memphis, and could quite possibly open up a whole other world for her if she was actually interested. As an artist who was always looking to improve in his craft, he deeply believed in an artist's need to grow. He knew he couldn't keep this opportunity away from Memphis—it wouldn't be right.

"You have my okay to talk to her about the project. If she's interested, I'll let her out of her contract long enough to do the movie," BJ said.

Legend stared back at him, her eyes reflecting her surprise, but then she nodded before standing and extending her hand.

"Thank you," she said. "That was much easier than I expected."

BJ grinned and nodded. "Well, you still have to sell it to Memphis."

"How's Allexx?" Legend asked.

"She's good," BJ said. "I'm surprised she's not knocking down your door to work on this film."

Legend grinned. "She's called me."

"Little sneak…" BJ said, grinning too.

"She's already committed to another film, so you're probably safe," she said, winking at him with a somewhat devilish expression.

BJ laughed.

It was well known in the Hollywood community that Legend Azaria had slept with more than a couple of the leading and/or supporting ladies in her films. She usually had at least one affair per film, lasting the length of the project. There had been a great deal of flirting going on between Allexxiss and Legend during their filming, but Legend had respected BJ Sparks far too much to cross that line. Besides, she had reasoned at the time, she liked her head where it was, and BJ

12

Sparks was no one to be messed with. Messing with Allexxiss Ramsey-Sparks was courting certain death and dismemberment by one Brenden James Sparks, in which Legend was not interested. Hence she had steered clear of any romantic entanglements with Allexxiss, while still coaxing an Academy Award–winning performance from her.

"Come on, Riley, push it!" Kai said sharply.

"I can't, I can't…" Sweat was dripping from Riley's face as she did her best to dig in for just a little more energy.

"Do it! Right now!" Kai yelled, her tone all drill sergeant.

Riley gave a yell of pure anger as she gritted her teeth and forced her muscles to do one more rep. It had been six weeks since she'd begged Kai, her daughter's girlfriend, to train her for a part in Legend Azaria's new movie. There were definitely times, like right now, when she regretted it.

"Good! Now bring it down slow…" Kai said, her voice trailing off. "Slow, Riley!"

Every muscle in her body was screaming, shaking and begging for her to stop; even so, she did what she was told, bringing the weights down slowly, feeling the searing, burning pain through her arms. Finally she set the bar on the poles. She saw Kai's hands above her, hovering in case she missed it.

"You did it!" Kai said, grinning. "I told you that you could."

"I hate you right now, Kai Temple, I really do," Riley said, sitting up and mopping her face with a towel.

"And how much are you going to love me when you get that

part?"

"More than my daughter does," Riley said, winking.

"Oh, I seriously doubt that," Kai said with a grin.

"You know," Riley said, "I'm really beginning to see the draw of you beautiful butches."

Kai rolled her eyes, shaking her head. "And what's that?"

"Hey, I see how my daughter walks around smiling all the time," Riley said seriously, "and you have everything to do with that, Kai. You take care of her."

"She takes care of me too. It's mutual."

Riley nodded. "I see that too. I've never seen Finley so happy—never."

"I'm glad," Kai said. "I want to make her happy."

"And that's the difference between you and everyone else she's ever dated. You want to make her happy—everyone else wants her to make them happy."

Kai looked back at her, hesitation clear on her face. "What are you saying to me?"

"I'm saying that you two need to make it permanent." Riley reached up to touch Kai on the cheek. "I'm saying I want you to make my daughter an honest woman."

Kai's lips curled into a grin. "So you're asking me to marry your daughter?"

"Unless you want to marry me instead," Riley said with a wink and a grin.

Kai chuckled, shaking her head. "I think you've overdosed on endorphins for the day."

Riley laughed. "You might be right about that one."

"So when do you see Legend Azaria about the part?" Kai asked as they made their way to the locker room so Riley could shower.

"I've got a meeting set with her for tomorrow." Riley stopped and turned to look up at Kai. "Do you think I'm ready?" she asked, her expression suddenly far less confident.

Kai studied Riley. She was wearing short bike shorts and a black tank top with a black exercise bra under it. Her face was devoid of makeup and her long, wavy blond hair was pulled back tight into a bun. Her arms and legs were cut with hard-won muscle; Kai couldn't detect an ounce of fat on her.

"What rifle do we carry?" Kai asked.

"M16."

"Where do we carry it?"

"Low and tight, finger to the side of the trigger guard, cocked and locked."

"What do we call the battlefield?"

"Outside the wire."

"What do you call a second lieutenant?"

"Boot lewy."

"Prepare to fire?"

"Lock and load."

"Go to bed?"

"Hit the rack."

"Take a piss?"

"Hit the head."

"The Navy."

"Is who the Marines call when they need a ride."

Kai nodded. "I think you're ready."

Riley grinned. "Oorah!"

Kai laughed. "Definitely ready."

"So you'll send me the bill, right?" Riley asked, her grin wide. "My accountant will need it."

Kai looked back at her for a long moment, then shook her head. "I don't charge family."

Riley's mouth fell open in shock. "Kai... you spent hours with me. I have to pay you. I know how much you make—you can't afford to hand out your time like that."

"I don't charge family," Kai repeated.

"I... You..." Riley stammered, her blue eyes reflecting her utter shock.

"Go shower," Kai said, nodding toward the locker room. "I'll clear up."

She was actually surprised when Riley walked up and hugged her tightly.

"Thank you for this, for everything," Riley said, her tone affected.

Never before in her life had someone given her something for nothing; there was always a price, no matter how obscure. Kai had given her time and her consideration. Kai Temple was one of a kind, that was for damned sure.

"Thank you for meeting with me," Legend said as she sat down with Memphis.

Memphis nodded, looking a bit perplexed. Kieran was with her, because Memphis had been completely unsure about this meeting. She had no idea why a movie director would want to talk to her.

"This is Kieran, my wife," she said, gesturing to the girl with the big blue eyes.

Legend nodded to Kieran, smiling. "Nice to meet you."

"You too," Kieran replied, her expression as cautious as Memphis'.

"England?" Legend queried.

Kieran smiled and nodded.

"Can you two please relax?" Legend asked, looking between the two of them and holding up a hand plaintively. "I swear this isn't a firing squad or anything."

Memphis grinned.

"Did you get a chance to read the synopsis of the story?" Legend asked her, looking at Kieran too when she saw that Memphis was holding on to her hand tightly.

Both women nodded.

"I just have no idea what you want with me," Memphis said.

Legend grinned, cheered by the completely unpolished answer. Memphis was genuine; she already liked that about her.

"I need someone to do the sound."

"I do sound for music—concerts, not movies," Memphis said, shaking her head.

"I checked you out," Legend said. "You have a degree in audio production, and I know they cover movie sound in those programs."

"Yeah, but…" Memphis said, trailing off as she once again shook her head.

"Look." Legend put her hand on the table in front of her, leaning forward in her desire to convince Memphis. "I'm looking to staff my crew with members of our own community, because I think it's about goddamned time we got back some of our own. I want you for this movie because I think you're damned talented, and I think you can apply that to anything, not just music. Besides, I'm going to need music too," she added.

"What are you thinking in terms of for music?" Memphis asked, her eyes sparkling with interest now.

Legend grinned. "I've been listening to a lot of Crüe and Van Halen. My latest obsession is *The Heroin Diaries* from Sixx:A.M."

Memphis looked surprised, but then nodded. "Dark," she said, her eyes widening slightly.

"Fairly," Legend agreed.

The Heroin Diaries was an almost autobiographical album that explored the dangers and insights found in addiction and redemption. It was very dark, and very powerful in its raw message.

Memphis nodded again, her expression flickering as if she sensed some underlying damage in the other woman.

"I can't guarantee I'll be any good at movie sound," she said, wanting to be completely honest with Legend. "And I am in a contract with Badlands Records."

"BJ and I have already talked. He's willing to let you out of your contract long enough to do the movie if you so choose."

Kieran and Memphis exchanged a glance. Legend noted they looked surprised.

"I'm not stupid enough to go up against BJ Sparks—not in person and definitely not in court," Legend said, grinning. "So, are you in?" she asked, her look at Memphis pointed.

Memphis still looked hesitant.

"Look, I have a bachelor's degree in film and media and a Master of Fine Arts in documentary and film from Stanford University," Legend said. "So I'm sure I can help you on the learning curve... but I don't have the instincts you have for sound—I need you."

Memphis' eyes had widened at the mention of Legend's degrees from a prestigious college. Her lips twitched at the notion of her instincts for sound; she didn't believe she had an instinct, she just loved it. She took a deep breath, blowing it out as she turned to Kieran. Kieran looked back at her, her blue eyes shining with confidence in her wife's ability.

"Come on," Legend said. "What have you got to lose?"

Memphis glanced back over at the dark-haired butch, searching Legend's face, trying to discern if there was any other reason she was offering the job. She couldn't detect anything covert.

"Okay, let's give it a shot," Memphis said finally.

Legend smiled broadly as she extended her hand. "Welcome to the movie business."

"Who's Legend Azaria?" Cat asked, looking back at a very excited Jovina.

"She's like the director to work with in Hollywood right now, Cat…"

"And she wants you to work on a screenplay?" Cat asked, pulling her gun out of the holster at her back and setting it on the dresser, her deep blue eyes still trained on Jovina. "Have you ever done a screenplay?"

"Yes, a couple, but never for anything like this," Jovina said, shaking her head in absolute wonder.

"No offense, babe, but why you?" Cat immediately held up her hands in a defensive gesture when Jovina narrowed her eyes dangerously at her. "I mean, if you've only got a small amount of experience, why would this 'hot director' want you to work on her film?"

Jovina pressed her lips together. She'd wondered the same thing, but she didn't like Cat pointing it out.

Setting down her badge, Cat walked over to where Jovina sat on their bed. She crawled onto the bed, her blond hair falling over her shoulder as she leaned in to capture Jovina's lips with her own. Jovina sighed, wrapping her arms around Cat's neck and pulling her closer. The conversation was forgotten at that point, as they kissed and Cat slowly removed their clothes. The fire between them caught, and they made love, exciting each other beyond all reason as they always did.

Afterward, Jovina lay next to Cat, her hand possessively on her stomach, her leg thrown over Cat's. Cat's arm was around Jovina, holding her to her intimately.

"I heard she approached Memphis too," Jovina said.

"For a movie?"

"The word is that she's trying to use only LGBT people."

"What's the movie about?"

"It's somewhat autobiographical, from what I understand. I can let you read the synopsis she sent over."

"Okay," Cat said, her natural suspicion as always on full blast.

Catalina had been a police officer and an undercover narcotics officer prior to being made a special agent supervisor for LA IMPACT, a task force division of the California Department of Justice. She came by suspicion naturally.

Jovina reached over to the nightstand and picked up the synopsis. It took Catalina ten minutes to read the five sheets of paper.

"So it's definitely a lesbian movie…" Cat said.

"Do you want to come to the meeting with me?" Jovina asked.

Cat looked pensive for a moment, narrowing her eyes slightly. "Are you okay with me being there?"

"You're better at reading people than I am."

Cat grinned. "Occupational hazard."

"And maybe my benefit," Jovina said. "If you don't think everything is right, you can stop me from making a mistake."

"What if she's just hot for ya?"

"Then you can shoot her and be done with it," Jovina replied, her dark eyes widening dramatically.

"Damned right," Cat said, pulling Jovina in to kiss her again. "The story's good, though," she added when their lips parted.

"I know. I'm actually kind of excited about working on it, if she's for real."

Cat nodded, hoping for Jovina's sake that Legend Azaria wasn't full of shit.

They found out the next day that Legend Azaria was very serious, and had every intention of making an Academy Award–winning movie.

"An Oscar for screenwriting could do your career a lot of good," she said to Jovina.

"Yeah, let's just keep our feet on the ground here, okay," Cat said, her look cynical.

Legend grinned at the hot blonde—she was tough, that was for sure. She liked that. Naturally, she'd noticed the gold badge clipped to Catalina Roché's belt, along with the nasty-looking gun on her hip. She was fairly certain those were on display for her benefit, and she liked that Catalina was that protective of her girlfriend. She'd heard that all of these women were connected in some way, shape, or form; she found it quite interesting.

"Either way, it'll make a nice paycheck," Legend said.

"I hope you understand I really don't have a lot of experience in screenwriting," Jovina said. "I've only written two other screenplays."

Legend shook her head. Did these women have no game or guile when it came to negotiating in Hollywood?

"I've read both of the screenplays you wrote, and I liked them. I think you translated the material well to the dialogue and stage direction."

"And you think I can do that with your story?" Jovina asked. "I

22

don't know a lot about the military."

Legend grinned. "Fortunately I spent ten years in it, so I do."

"So you plan to be involved in the work on the screenplay," Jovina said.

"I plan to be involved in every aspect of the movie. This movie is my life—I need it to come out right."

"So it is autobiographical?" Cat asked, her dark blue eyes searching Legend's face.

"What are you looking for?" Legend asked her. "Trying to decide if I'm for real here?"

"Pretty much," Cat replied, her tone all cop.

Legend sat up from her relaxed position, taking off her shades and looking straight into Cat's eyes.

"I'm as real as I can possibly be on this one, Agent Roché."

Cat stared back at her, noting the direct look and the shadows contained in Legend's eyes as well as the dark circles under them.

"When's the last time you slept, Ms. Azaria?" she asked.

"It's Legend," the dark-haired butch said, putting her glasses back on and sitting back. "And it's been a few days. I tend to hyperfocus when something's important."

Cat nodded, wondering where Legend got the energy to keep going and betting she knew. She was convinced that if she searched Legend Azaria right then she'd find speed on her, though there weren't a lot of telltale signs. She was wearing a short-sleeved T-shirt, but her arms were also covered in tatt sleeves—easier to hide track marks, if that was how she got high…

23

Legend felt Cat's penetrating stare and knew she was pushing her luck yet again, sitting across from a narc when she was holding. It was part of the challenge, part of the high. She was fairly certain she wasn't fooling Catalina Roché, but she was hoping that Jovina's desire to do the movie would override the narc's need to make a bust. Calculated risks—Legend lived on them.

"Well, Ms. Azevedo, are you in?" Legend asked.

"I have to ask," Jovina said. "Why me?"

A grin played at Legend's lips. These women took nothing for granted, did they? "Because I want *family* on this," she said simply.

"There are no other gay screenwriters?" Cat asked.

"Men, yes," Legend said. "I don't think gay men get lesbians and the way we talk to each other—do you?"

Cat looked back at Legend, sensing that she was very serious and that she was committed to the project she was selling. Cat had checked the woman out; she was very definitely a serious player in Hollywood. Even BJ Sparks respected her, and Cat took that pretty seriously. She glanced at Jovina, who was looking to her for her opinion. Narrowing her eyes slightly because she still had reservations about Legend, but seeing easily that Jovina was dying to say yes, Cat gave a slight nod.

Jovina smiled immediately, looking over at Legend. "I'm in."

"Excellent," Legend said, glancing first at Cat, then at Jovina as she stood. She extended her hand. "Welcome aboard."

Riley walked up to the doors to the sprawling mansion on Malibu beach. This meeting had been scheduled and rescheduled three times; she was beginning to wonder if Legend Azaria just wasn't interested in her and was hoping she'd get tired of being put off.

After knocking on the door, she glanced around, noting the gray slate tile in a zigzag pattern on the wall of the entry, where she could see through the glass of the front door. She thought it was an interesting design choice for a beach house. She was doing anything to distract herself from her nervousness. It was odd that the meeting had been set for the director's own home; usually they preferred people not knowing where they lived, especially much sought-after directors like Legend Azaria.

A diminutive girl who looked about twenty, with a short, dark bob haircut and thick-rimmed glasses on her huge eyes, answered the door. She held a clipboard, looking quite efficient.

"Riley Taylor to see Ms. Azaria," Riley said when the girl simply looked at her oddly.

"Yes, Ms. Taylor. I'm Tula, Legend's assistant. Come in, please."

Riley walked in. The house was nice, very open and light. The entire western side of it was all windows, to capture multiple views of the beach, only steps from the back.

"Legend hasn't slept for four days," Tula said, as if reporting on the weather. "She's fallen asleep in her room, but she told me that when you arrived I was to send you up."

"Well, should we reschedule…" Riley said, thinking this was just another put-off, although a creative one. Who didn't sleep for four days?

"No, Legend told me I was not to reschedule you again. She was rather vehement on the subject," Tula said, blinking a couple of times. "So, please, go up these stairs. Legend's room is the last door on the right."

Riley looked back at the girl. Surely she was kidding. "You want me to go wake up the director of the movie I'm asking for a part in?" she asked, dumbfounded.

Tula nodded.

"Does she sleep armed?" Riley muttered as she started up the stairs.

"Not anymore," Tula called after her.

Riley started laughing, thinking this had to be the most ridiculous situation she'd ever been in—and for someone who'd been in Hollywood since she was five, that was saying a lot. At the door to Legend Azaria's room, Riley paused.

"This is insane," she whispered to herself, reaching up to knock.

There was no answer.

"Seriously?" Riley muttered.

Trying the handle, she found it was unlocked. She carefully opened the door, wondering if there'd be a news story later that night about how actress Riley Taylor had been killed when she was mistaken for a burglar by hot new director Legend Azaria.

Shaking her head even as she stepped into the darkened room, Riley thought she was going to have a hell of a story to tell, in any case. She waited for her eyes to adjust, then looked around. The curtains were drawn, so it was especially dark. The only illumination came from the bathroom, where a light had been left on. She looked to her left and saw Legend Azaria.

The first thing she noticed about Legend was how strong a jawline she had—a strong, handsome jawline, she thought, much like

Kai's. Legend had a somewhat darker skin tone, and Riley noticed the cut of her black hair, very short on the sides and long on top. It was also evident how slim the director was. She wore a black tank top and extremely faded and tattered jeans. Her feet were bare. She lay with her arms up over her head, her chin tilted up.

"Ms. Azaria?" Riley said softly, not wanting to startle the other woman.

Legend didn't move. Walking closer, Riley tried again.

"Ms. Azaria?"

Again, Legend didn't move.

She sleeps rather soundly, doesn't she?

Riley stepped even closer, staring down at the director, seeing what a seriously handsome face the woman had. She reached out, touching Legend's arm and calling her name again.

This time Legend stirred, opening her eyes and looking up at Riley, her expression understandably vacant for a moment. She blinked a couple of times, moving to sit up and rubbing her face.

"Ms. Taylor, thanks for coming. Sorry about... this," Legend said, gesturing to her bedroom. "I've been burning it heavily for days—couldn't stay awake any longer."

"I understand," Riley said.

Legend looked back at her for a long moment, taking in the long hair, the makeup, the perfectly tailored clothing. She shook her head.

"I'm sorry I wasted your time," she said. "But you're not right for the movie."

"Ms. Azaria—" Riley began.

"It's Legend."

"Legend," Riley said. "I don't think you understand how much I want this part."

"You're trying for the part of Lizette?"

Riley nodded. "Yes. I've put a lot of time into learning what I need to know for the part."

"Did you read the synopsis of the story?" Legend asked, her expression doubtful.

"Yes."

"Lizette's butch, Ms. Taylor—you're about the farthest thing I've ever seen from butch," Legend said, putting her knees up to her chest, her arms over them with her tattoos on full display.

"I understand that," Riley said. "And certainly you understand that hair and makeup can be changed."

Legend looked back at her, her tongue up over her front teeth, her eyes widening at Riley's assertion. "Haven't seen a makeup artist yet that can make a complete femme into a butch."

"Then I guess you never saw Charlize Theron in *Monster*."

Legend's lips curled into a grin. The woman was feisty, she would give her that. She narrowed her eyes at Riley, her stare downright invasive, but Riley stood there, refusing to flinch or give her the satisfaction of making her look away. Instead she stared at the director, withstanding her scrutiny.

"Go wash off all that makeup and pull back all that hair," Legend said, circling her finger in the general direction of Riley's face and then gesturing to the master bathroom.

Riley narrowed her eyes, but she turned on her heel in a fair imitation of a military pivot and all but marched into the bathroom to do as she'd been directed.

Legend reached over to turn on her bedside lamp, grinning. Riley Taylor would be a major asset to the film, as well known as she was, but she was damned if she was going to water down her movie to put a "star" in it. She either fit the part or she didn't, and if she didn't she wasn't going to be in the movie—it was as simple as that.

When Riley emerged from the master bathroom she had shed her tailored jacket, exposing a navy blue tank top and arms that had an admirable amount of definition to them. She'd washed off her makeup, and her hair was back in a neat but not overly elegant bun. She stood next to the bed, looking down at Legend pointedly.

"And what do you think you know for the part?" Legend asked wryly.

"I've been working with a trainer who is a former Marine. She's taught me things about being a Marine, such as how to field strip an M16 rifle."

Legend couldn't help but grin at the image of the beautiful blonde stripping an M16. "How long was she in the Marines?"

"Fourteen years. She's actually my daughter-in-law, basically."

"She's dating your son?" Legend asked mildly.

"Daughter."

Legend's eyes widened slightly, her lips curling into a grin again. "So you're around lesbians, and likely a butch, and that makes you think you're qualified to be one in my movie?"

"No, the fact that I have five Academy Awards for my acting

makes me qualified," Riley replied, her tone devoid of pleading. "My association with Kai and my daughter's friends notwithstanding."

Legend gazed back at Riley for another long moment. It was niggling at the back of her head how much she looked like her... It set her foot to moving, the thought of that...

"You're totally wrong for Lizette," she said finally. "Would you be interested in reading for the part of Georgia?"

Riley opened her mouth to refuse, but then stopped. Georgia was a key character in the movie as well. Although not the main character, she was in the entire movie. It was clear Legend Azaria wouldn't even consider her for the part of Lizette, but maybe Georgia was an acceptable compromise.

"Yes," she said finally.

Legend nodded. "Fine. Be in my studio tomorrow at ten a.m. I'll messenger over the scene you'll read for."

"I can do that," Riley said.

"Then I'll see you tomorrow," Legend said, moving to lie back down.

Riley shook her head. The woman was an enigma, and certainly not what she was used to in Hollywood. As she left the room and walked down the stairs, she knew that Legend had expected her to refuse to read for a part. Someone of her status didn't do that anymore, but she was willing to do whatever it took to get a part in this movie.

Later that day, when she received the scene she was to read for, she was surprised to note that it was one in which she'd need to kiss another woman. In a panic, she immediately went to see Kai and Finley.

"What is it?" Finley asked as she answered the door at Kai's.

"I have to read for that part tomorrow, and I have to kiss another woman," Riley said.

Finley started laughing immediately; even Kai grinned at the panic on Riley's face.

"Oh, you two!" Riley said, giving them both a foul look. "It's not something I've ever done!"

"Lips are lips, Mom," Finley said. "You didn't think you'd have to kiss another woman or be naked around another woman in the movie?"

"Well, yes, I thought of that," Riley said. "But that would be after I have the part—this is before that."

"Sounds to me like you better get used to it fast," Kai said wryly.

"Okay, you need to kiss me," Riley said.

"Uh…" Kai stammered, shaking her head.

"Mom!" Finley exclaimed. "You are not kissing Kai!"

"How else am I supposed to get past this block?"

"Gonna have to get in touch with your inner lesbian," Kai said, her dark eyes widening.

"Right, sure…" Riley said, shaking her head.

Finley smiled. "Women's lips are awesome. Just go for it, don't think about gay or straight—think awesome kiss."

"You sure you won't kiss me?" Riley asked Kai.

"My girlfriend has issues with that kind of thing, me kissing other women…" Kai said, winking at Finley.

"Especially my mother, for God's sake!"

"You are no help at all, Finley, my love," Riley said, patting her daughter on the cheek.

"Not sharing my girlfriend, Mom," Finley said with a grin. "You'd just fall in love and I'd have to kill you."

Chapter 2

They'd been hanging out a lot since meeting. Georgette was forever finding Legend on the field, running. It was what Legend did when things pissed her off; she ran until she was too tired to get herself in trouble. One day during a mission, however, she was caught by some shrapnel from an exploding IED, just barely. She was more excited about the fact that she'd filmed the explosion; fortunately, no one else was hurt. She'd been patient enough for the medic to remove the pieces of shrapnel from her cheek and next to her eye and then let him clean it, and then she was gone. Heading to her barracks, she pulled out her camera and rolled back the footage. She was still looking at it when Georgette came in. She was alone, because it was only a two-room barracks set aside for female personnel. She was the only one in it at that point.

"Oh my God! I heard you were hurt!" Georgette said, sitting on the bunk next to Legend, searching her face.

"I'm fine," Legend said, flicking her fingers toward the injuries with no concern whatsoever.

"Let me see that," Georgette said, taking Legend's face in her hands and turning her head.

Legend rolled her eyes and withstood Georgette's ministrations.

"See? Fine," Legend said when Georgette finally released her face.

Georgette gave her a cynical look, but nodded. "So what did you get?" she asked, moving closer so she could see the screen on the camera.

"IED explosion," Legend said, grinning.

"I hate you so much..." Georgette muttered.

Legend played the footage, and Georgette excitedly hugged her. "That's so amazing! You're so damned lucky you weren't killed!"

"Yeah, yeah, I know."

They talked long into the night about various topics. At one point they were lying across Legend's bunk. Georgette turned over on her side, facing Legend. She looked like she wanted to ask something, but she didn't.

"What?" Legend asked.

"Nothing," Georgette said, shaking her head.

"Seriously, what?"

Georgette pressed her lips together. "The rule says I can't," she said simply.

"You can't... ask," Legend said, understanding dawning. "And I can't tell..." she added pointedly.

Georgette nodded. "You know I'm not, right?" she said.

"Nobody's perfect," Legend said, grinning.

Georgette laughed. "I'm from a good, old-fashioned, Bible-thumping family. They'd completely lose their minds!"

"Well, my family doesn't know, which is the only reason I'm still a member of it."

"Do you have a big family?"

"Pretty big," Legend said. "Israelis tend to be rather prolific."

"You use a lot of big words," Georgette said. "Did you go to college?"

"Yeah. I went to Stanford."

"Holy cow! That's, like, Ivy League, isn't it?"

"I suppose. I went there because they had the best cinematography program in the West."

"This stuff's really important to you."

"All I've ever wanted to do."

"It's great that you're getting to do it."

"What did you want to do when you joined?" Legend asked.

"I wanted to be a radio communications specialist."

"So why not try for it?"

"Because my commander doesn't believe in women knowing too much."

"Because he's a fucking asshat."

Georgette grinned at that.

In the end, Georgette finally left around midnight. They'd had a good, long talk, and Legend was happy that someone knew about her being gay. She trusted Georgette to keep her secret.

Two weeks later, Georgette spent the evening in her barracks again. They talked long into the night, because Georgette was really tired of her job and wanted a change. Legend was trying to encourage her to ask for a transfer.

"Why would they let me?" Georgette asked.

"Because you're smart and capable. Why else?" Legend said.

"What if they don't think so."

"You're a Marine—that says so."

Georgette looked back at her, seeing the set of her mouth and thinking she'd love to be that sure of things. Then, suddenly, she was really looking at Legend's lips, and she felt something stir inside of her. She tried to ignore it—it wasn't the first time it had happened. So often when Legend would come in from the track and lie on the infield area, she would strip off her tank top down to her jog bra, and Georgette would find herself staring and feeling that stir.

Legend noticed Georgette's expression and sensed what was going on. She moved to sit up, but Georgette's hand on her shoulder stopped her.

"Will you kiss me?" Georgette asked.

Legend looked back at her, blinking a couple of times. Sure, she'd thought the blonde was hot; sure, she'd have gone for it if she'd been gay, but she wasn't. Being gay in the Marines was the single hardest thing Legend had ever done—she certainly wasn't going to sign anyone up for that kind of hassle.

"Why?" Legend asked.

"Because I want you to," Georgette said, moving closer.

Legend steeled herself. It had been way too long since she'd been with anyone, and Georgette was really beautiful, even without makeup, even with her hair back…

"George…" she began, wanting desperately to find something else to focus on so she wouldn't do what she really wanted to do.

"Just kiss me, Legend, please… I need to know…"

"Need to know what?" Legend asked, but her breath was coming *fast now, her heart pounding. Georgette was so close…*

"I need to know why I want to kiss you all the time," Georgette said, so innocent in what she was saying, and having no idea of the effect she was having on Legend's self-control. "Why I look at your lips and can't think of anything else…"

"Please don't ask me to do this, George."

"I have to. Who else am I going to ask? Please, Legend," she said again, moving even closer, her body pressing against Legend's now.

It was a simple move to lower her head, and their lips touched immediately. Georgette sighed, and Legend was undone. She slid her hand behind Georgette's head, pulling her closer and deepening the kiss as a riot of sensations coursed through her body. Georgette's hand at her waist made it all that harder to pull her lips from the other woman's.

"George, we can't… we can't…" Legend said, shaking her head.

"Why?" Georgette asked, so plaintively that Legend grimaced.

"Because being gay in the military is the stupidest thing you can possibly do. Just forget this, okay? Just forget it." Legend moved away to sit on the other side of her bunk, her back to Georgette.

She couldn't look at her. She didn't want to see the rejection on her face, or whatever else might be there. She practically held her breath until she heard Georgette get up and leave. As soon as the barracks door closed, she flung herself back on her bed, thinking she'd just managed to lose her best friend in the process of avoiding a liaison.

"Great move, Azaria. Just brilliant…" she muttered.

Riley walked into the studio. It was quiet, and she wondered if she had the wrong place. Turning a corner, she saw Legend Azaria sitting in a chair, her skinny-jean-clad legs wide apart, her booted feet planted sturdily. Her back was to Riley, and Riley could see that she had headphones in her ears. She could actually hear the music, it was so loud. It was obvious that Legend was very into whatever song it was that she was listening to. Her head was moving to the beat, and she was soundlessly singing the words; Riley could lipread "Pray for me."

Walking over, she made a point of moving to where Legend could see her.

"Oh," Legend said, reaching up and pulling out one of the earbuds, the music blaring from it.

"You'll go deaf, listening to it that loud," Riley observed.

"Hasn't happened yet," Legend replied mildly as she turned the song off.

"Am I early?" Riley asked, looking around.

"No. I don't need to decide things in a committee, so it's just you and me."

"Who am I supposed to read with?"

"Well, I just said it's just you and me, so what do you think?" Legend asked evenly.

"So I'm reading with you?" Riley asked dumbly, already panicking again about the kissing thing. She'd have to kiss the damned director of the movie?"

"You catch on quick."

"I…" Riley stammered. "Oh, sorry. Yes, of course."

Legend grinned, noting how nervous Riley was. She had a feeling she knew exactly why, and it amused her no end. The woman wanted to be in a lesbian movie, in a role as a lesbian, but she was nervous about having to kiss a woman? Was she actually crazy?

Legend got up, noting that Riley's face was devoid of makeup and her hair was pulled back. At least she'd remembered that part.

"We'll do it standing up," Legend said, purposely allowing the double entendre to set in before she continued. "Since there's no bed around," she said, her light eyes sparkling. "Unless you'd like me to find one," she added, her look almost predatory.

Riley's eyes widened, but then she realized what Legend was doing. She was damned if she was going to be intimidated out of this part. She drew on every single ounce of courage she'd ever had and looked back at her.

"I can do you standing, sitting, or wherever," she said pointedly.

Legend took a step back as if she'd actually been pushed, even as a grin curled her lips. The woman had balls, she'd give her that.

"Touché," she said, inclining her head.

Riley smiled, glad that she'd been able to best the director, even if it was only momentarily.

"We can begin whenever you're ready," Legend said.

Riley nodded, moving closer to Legend—a foot away, like the scene called for. She closed her eyes for a moment, conjuring up the image of the scene in her head. When she opened them she could see the barracks, the bed neatly made, and herself with the character of Lizette, who looked exactly like Legend Azaria, in front of her. They'd been talking for hours, like they had so many times before.

"What if they won't let me try for it?" Riley said, her expression worried.

"Why wouldn't they?" Legend replied.

"Because they don't think I'm good enough," Riley said, looking like she believed what they thought.

"You're good enough to be a Marine—that's good enough."

Riley stared back at Legend, her eyes searching, then centered on Legend's lips. They were slightly pursed, twitching slightly in her agitation at the way the men in the Marines treated women. They were such sexy lips, just full enough without being overly so. Riley's lips parted, as if anticipating the kiss she wanted.

Legend started to move away. Riley reached out, touching her shoulder, stopping her.

"Would you kiss me?" she asked breathlessly.

"Why?"

"Because I need to know."

"What do you think you need to know?" Legend asked, her voice low.

Riley moved closer, her eyes connecting with Legend's. "I need to know why I want you to kiss me all the time, and why when I look at your lips I can't think of anything else..." Her eyes went to Legend's lips again, lips that were now trembling.

Legend raised her chin, grimacing as if in pain. "Please don't ask me to do this..." she said, her voice a soft plea.

"I have to," Riley said, pressing closer, her lips so close to Legend's now. "Please..."

Hazel eyes connected with blue ones, and then Riley felt the softness of Legend's lips, with just enough strength behind them to part her own. She closed her eyes, moaning softly as those lips moved over hers expertly, and felt Legend's hand come up to hold the back of her head. Time froze.

Suddenly Legend was pulling away, her eyes inexplicably glazed with tears, and she was shaking her head.

"I can't, I can't…" she chanted, moving away from Riley and bending over, her hands on her thighs, breathing so heavily Riley was afraid she was going to pass out.

"Legend, are you okay?" Riley asked, touching her back.

Legend nodded, still breathing heavily, closing her eyes.

"I'm sorry," she said, shaking her head. "I'm sorry… That was… Fuck…" She moved to kneel as tears slipped from her eyes.

Riley crouched next to her, not understanding what was happening but feeling like she needed to try to help. She put her hand on her shoulder, smoothing the material of her shirt from her neck to the edge of her shoulder and then back again.

"Was that scene… real?" Riley asked.

Legend nodded as she continued to try and get her breathing under control.

"This is really hard for you, isn't it?"

"Harder than I realized it would be," Legend said in a moment of pure honesty.

Riley pressed her lips together, only able to imagine how hard it would be.

Legend reached up, wiping at her eyes with the back of her hand, doing her best to compose herself again. She got up, and held her hand out to Riley to help her up as well. Riley took it, getting to her feet and staring at Legend. Legend grinned, keeping hold of her hand.

"You got it," she said with a smile.

"I got the part?" Riley asked.

Legend laughed. "You catch on quick, huh?"

Riley laughed too. "I guess not so much around you."

"You'll get used to me."

"It will be a pleasure, I'm sure."

"Don't count on that," Legend said, shaking her head, her grin still in place.

Kai and Finley were sleeping when Kai's phone chimed. She moaned tiredly and reached over, picking it up and looking at the message.

"Shit…" she muttered.

"Hmm?" Finley murmured.

Kai grimaced. This was the last thing she'd expected, and the last thing she wanted to have to tell Finley.

"Babe, what is it?" Finley asked when Kai didn't answer.

Kai blew her breath out. "I'm getting called up."

"What does that mean?" Finley asked, perplexed.

"It means my reserve unit is being deployed."

Finley sat up. "Deployed where?"

Kai shook her head. "I don't know. The official orders aren't in yet—we've just been notified to report."

"No," Finley said, shaking her head.

"Fin…" Kai began, sitting up.

"No, Kai!" she said sharply. "No, they can't just… No!"

"Babe, it's part of being a reserve."

"I don't care. They can't… You give them a weekend a month, that's all—that's all…" Finley knew she wasn't making sense, and the tears started.

Kai pulled her into her arms. Finley fought her, but Kai just tightened her grip until she gave in, crying.

Kai's phone chimed again, and she picked it up with one hand, still holding Finley with the other. She checked the message.

"Remi's unit got called up too."

"Jesus…" Finley whispered, wondering how Wynter was handling the news.

"Oh hell fucking no, Remi! You tell them no!" Wynter yelled as she paced back and forth in their bedroom.

Remington lay on their bed, watching Wynter, her expression mild as always, even in the face of Wynter's yelling. Wynter stopped, turning to Remington, her hands on her hips.

"Call them right now," she said. "They can't have you. You gave them eight fucking years in the Middle East—that's enough!"

"That's not how it works, babe," Remington said evenly.

"Then tell them you're quitting the reserves as of now!"

Remington pressed her lips together, then parted them in a gesture that meant she was getting annoyed. Wynter saw it, and it made her mad again.

"You're going to pick them over me?"

Remington didn't answer, merely looking back at her.

"No answer?"

"I'm not going to answer a ridiculous question, Wynter," Remington said. "Come here."

"No," Wynter said stubbornly.

Remington's face was serious as she tilted her head slightly at her fiancée. "Come here," she said again.

Wynter looked mutinous, but she knew it wasn't going to do her any good to try to avoid letting Remington comfort her. Finally she blew her breath out in a rush and walked over to the bed, crawling onto it and into Remington's arms.

"I hate the Marines," Wynter said.

"I know," Remington said, her lips against Wynter's forehead.

"I hate them."

"Got it."

Wynter looked up at Remington, her eyes searching. "I can't lose you. If I—" she began, but Remington's hand on her mouth stopped her.

"You can't say that," Remington said seriously. "You can't put that out in the atmosphere. Don't ever say that."

Wynter's lips trembled, and then the tears started. It tore at Remington's heart, but she knew she had a duty and she knew she had to do it. It was a rough morning that only got worse when Remington texted Memphis to ask her to come by when she and Kieran had time.

Memphis' devastated look when she told her was another punch to the gut. Even though Memphis did her best to hold it together, it was obvious she was completely terrified. And before long she was running to the bathroom and throwing up, something she hadn't done for months. Memphis had an extreme sensitivity to stress; it manifested itself in twisting her stomach into knots until she had to throw up to relieve the pain.

On the other side of town, Kai was getting a completely different reaction from Cassiana.

"You're being deployed?" she asked.

Kai nodded.

"Where to?" Cassiana took a bite of the bagel she'd just fixed herself.

Kai grinned, glancing at Finley and noting the shocked look on her face. "Don't know yet. Final orders haven't come through."

Cassiana nodded. "That's usually within twenty-four hours of the post orders, right?"

"Usually, yes," Kai said, smiling proudly.

"Maybe it's somewhere cool," Cassiana said, her eyes widening.

"Guess we'll see."

Cassiana nodded. "Yep."

Later, in the car, Finley glanced over at Kai. "I don't get it."

"What?"

"Why Cass is so okay with this. What am I missing?"

Kai reached over, taking Finley's hand and kissing the back of it.

"You're missing that military brat gene, babe."

"So she's used to moving around, so you being deployed isn't a big deal?"

"Pretty much. She knows that it's part of military life."

Finley looked pensive, only nodding in response.

A party for Remington and Kai was quickly thrown together and held at the Club. Their final orders had come through, and they were being sent to Italy, which relieved both Finley and Wynter; the idea that their women could get sent back to the Middle East had terrified both of them. The group turned out in full force.

"Are you sure this is a good idea?" Legend asked Riley.

Riley smiled. "It's a great idea."

They'd been spending a lot of time together since her audition. Legend was working with her on preparation for the role and including her in the some of the planning. Riley found that she really liked Legend; the woman was dedicated to her craft in a way that was rare in Hollywood lately. They talked about the location plans and the various parts of the story. Legend had just finally settled on a leading lady for the movie; Talon Valois would play Lizette, opposite Riley. Talon was a rarity in Hollywood. At the age of twenty-nine, she was a chameleon; she could be anything a director wanted. Femme, butch, fat, thin; she could play a biker or a debutante. Her read for the part of Lizette had been amazing, and there'd been no doubt in Legend's mind that she could pull it off.

"And I'm a thousand years old compared to her," Riley had said, rolling her eyes.

"You don't look anywhere near fifty, Ri," Legend said. "If I hadn't known that you've been in Hollywood and films forever, I'd never have guessed it."

Riley had taken heart in what Legend had said. She knew Legend was dedicated to the authenticity of this movie, and that she wouldn't have put her in the role if she hadn't believed she could pull it off. The truth was, Riley Taylor knew how to take care of herself, and she didn't look anywhere near fifty. Sure, she had facials and chemical peels to keep age off her face, but she'd never had plastic surgery, and she was proud of that fact. Thanks to Kai and her regimen of healthy eating and exercise, Riley was in the best shape of her life, and she intended to keep it that way.

Now they were on their way to Kai and Remington's party. Riley had invited Legend, wanting her to meet Finley and Kai and the rest of their group. Riley had managed to meet most of them before, and really liked the people that Finley had become friends with. They were good people.

"Besides, you already know Jovina and Memphis," Riley added.

"That means Jovina's narc girlfriend'll be there…" Legend said, trailing off as she shook her head.

Riley glanced over at her. "You're not high, are you?" she asked, her tone completely free of judgment.

Legend's lips twitched. "No. Doesn't mean I don't have anything on me though."

"They aren't going to randomly search you at a party, Legend."

Legend grinned. "I dunno. Cat Roché probably thought about it a couple of times the first time I met her."

Riley gave her a narrowed look. "They have to have what's called probable cause."

"You learn that from *Law and Order*?" Legend asked, grinning.

Riley laughed. "Yep!"

Legend was driving her black old-school muscle car, and Riley couldn't help but think it really fit her personality. She was old school, tough, and edgy all at the same time. It was impossible to believe the woman was forty-four; she looked about thirty. She did listen to some fairly heavy rock music too.

As Legend entered the freeway toward West Hollywood, another song began on the stereo, and Riley paid attention to the lyrics, since Legend was singing them rather vehemently. The song was called "Pray For Me."

The chorus went, "Pray for me, cause I don't want to, pray for me, if you love me, cross your heart and hope that I won't die before the best day of my life... Just pray for me tonight..."

"That's the song you were listening to that day in the studio, isn't it?" Riley asked.

Legend nodded as she continued to sing.

"Who is this?" Riley asked, not recognizing the singer's voice.

"Sixx:A.M.," Legend said, then saw Riley's blank look. "Nikki Sixx from Mötley Crüe, he was the bassist. This is his band."

Riley nodded. "It sounds, um, rather... dark."

The song talked about dying a lot.

"This isn't anything," Legend said, grinning. "The album is called *The Heroin Diaries*. It's about drug use and ODing, and trying to come out the other side."

Riley widened her eyes. "Okay, really, really dark."

Legend nodded. "Whenever I work on a film, I center on a type of music—an album, a band, a style… This is the one I'm focused on now."

Riley nodded. As the next song started, it was obviously from the same band. The first line was "I don't want to die, out here in the valley…" She grimaced; it was very dark, and she wondered how dark the film was likely to get.

She'd already developed a concern about Legend. It was obvious to her that she was very deep into the movie, the title of which had been set as *For the Telling*, a play on the Don't Ask, Don't Tell law for the military. Legend's reaction to the scene they'd read for Riley's audition had been so strong. Riley worried how much it would affect her.

She'd heard a lot about Legend since she'd been interested in being in her movie. Legend Azaria was known for being completely immersed in a project. She wrapped herself up in the characters, the dialogue, the feel of the film, the sets, the places—everything. She was well known for going days without sleep, and for throwing complete fits when actors or actresses were unprofessional enough to be late to the set, or not put their everything into the role. She'd fired well-known actors and actresses for what she called "prima donna bullshit"; she didn't put up with it. She'd been quoted as saying, "If you want to work with me, you better bring your A game, because I don't do B game." She meant every word. She always brought her A game; she gave everything she had to a film, to the point where she would be wrecked for weeks afterward. She expected just as much dedication from everyone working with her.

49

They arrived at the Club and went inside. The group had taken over for the night, and had invited people they'd chosen from the regular crowd. Riley walked over to where Finley and Kai stood at one of the tables.

"Finley, Kai," she said, gesturing to Legend, "this is Legend Azaria. Legend, this is my daughter, Finley, and her girlfriend, Kai Temple."

Legend extended her hand to Finley, thinking the daughter was every bit as beautiful as her mother.

"Good to meet you," she said, smiling.

"You too," Finley said, taking in the handsome director. "My mother says a lot of really great things about you."

"That's 'cause she doesn't know me too well yet," Legend said, winking.

Finley laughed.

Legend looked at Kai then, easily seeing the Marine in her and appreciating it.

Kai extended her hand. "Azaria?" she queried. "Israeli?"

"Half, yes."

"That was fun with the Marines, huh?" Kai asked, knowing full well how much shit anyone of Middle Eastern descent would take from military personnel.

Legend laughed. "You got it. Should have heard them with my given name."

"Which is?" Kai asked.

"Ustura."

"That would have given any clerk I've ever met fits."

"And my CO."

"Hence, Legend?"

Legend shrugged. "It's the English translation, and it seemed easier."

"Didn't go back to the given after?"

"Got used to Legend by that time."

"How many years in?"

"Ten. I hear you got fourteen?"

"And counting," Kai said, rolling her eyes.

"Where they sending you?" Legend asked.

"Italy. Earthquake search, rescue, and clean-up."

"Search?" Legend asked, confused.

"K9s."

"Aw," Legend said. "Damned helpful, the canine Marines."

Kai grinned.

Riley had introduced Legend to others in the group, and she was starting to get edgy with all the cops she was meeting, including the director for the Division of Law Enforcement herself, Jericho Tehrani. They did have the Middle Eastern descent in common, however, so it went a little easier.

"I think I need a serious drink," Legend said. "What are you having?"

"White wine," Riley said.

"You got it." Legend strolled over to the bar.

Cat, Jericho, Rayden, and Kashena watched her cross the room. The dark-haired director was wearing all black, right down to her combat-style boots.

"Speed, right?" Cat said, glancing at the other three.

"Probably," Kashena said. "But not heavy duty."

"No," Rayden said. "Not hardcore, but…"

"She's not high now," Jericho said confidently.

"No, no one's that good at hiding it," Cat said.

"Bet she's holding, though," Kashena said.

Rayden nodded. "Oh yeah."

"What kind of trouble are you four up to?" Finley asked as she passed the four women.

"Assessing your mother's friend's drug use," Cat said.

Finley looked back at the four of them, not surprised.

"I wondered that myself," she said. "But I haven't seen any evidence that she's high right now."

"No, she's not," Kashena said. "But you can damned sure bet she uses. Cat says she said she hadn't slept for four days—you don't do that naturally."

"No, you don't," Finley said, glancing over at her mother, wondering if Riley knew about it. "You don't think she shoots it, do you?"

"Not seeing tracks, but those sleeves could hide it if she's careful," Cat said.

Finley was worried. She knew her mother liked Legend, and if she didn't know about the drug use it could cause problems.

"This is Hollywood," she said, not terribly surprised to hear that a director as dynamic as it sounded like Legend Azaria was used drugs.

Jericho nodded, her expression even. "Still illegal, Fin."

"I know," Finley said. "But—"

"Don't worry," Cat said. "We're not looking to bust her. We're just observing."

"Can't put the badges away tonight?" Finley asked, smiling.

"Twenty-four-seven, Fin," Kashena said, shaking her head.

Finley blew her breath out. "I do not want an incident here tonight."

Cat grinned. "Unless she breaks out her stash and starts handing it out, we'll be fine."

"Good," Finley said, giving her a narrowed look. "You're okay with her working with Jovina?"

"As long as she keeps the shit away from Jovi…" Cat said. "Jovi has a history with drugs, and if I think for a second Legend Azaria is offering her any, I'll fucking arrest her myself."

Finley nodded, seeing a side of Catalina Roché she'd never seen before. Catalina was one of the most changeable lesbians Finley had ever met. She could be completely feminine one minute, with hair done, makeup perfect, and a sexy outfit, and then very butch the next, when she was doing her job. It had always been interesting to Finley how Cat balanced that.

Later that night, Finley had an opportunity to talk to Legend. They were standing side by side at the bar, waiting for the bartender to get them drinks.

"My mother tells me you have a degree from Stanford?" Finley asked.

"Two, actually," Legend said.

"Really?" Finley asked, her eyes widening. "In?"

"I have a bachelor's in film and media and an MFA in documentary and film."

"Wow," Finley said. "That's pretty impressive."

"Not so much," Legend said, grinning. "Your mother said you got your medical degree from Harvard—now that's impressive."

Finley smiled. "We'll have to agree to disagree on that one."

Legend smiled, inclining her head. As their drinks were put up, Legend pulled out her credit card even as Finley took out cash. Legend put her hand over Finley's, halting her action.

"I got it," she said. "Gotta buy the Marine a drink or two."

Finley laughed. "Thank you."

They walked back over to the table and Legend handed Riley her drink. Finley handed Kai her shot and beer.

"Courtesy of Legend," she said.

Kai held the shot up to Legend, who held hers up as well.

"To our wives and lovers," Legend said with a grin.

"May they never meet," Kai said, laughing.

"Oorah!" Legend exclaimed.

"Oorah!"

They both did their shots.

Finley looked pointedly at Kai.

"It's an infantry thing," Kai said, smiling at Legend.

"I heard that," Remington said as she joined them. "And someone missed my shot…"

"Three more, coming up," Legend said as she reached out to gently grab a waitress. "Hey, beautiful, can you get my two Marines here a double shot of tequila, and one more for me? Thank you," she said with an engaging smile.

The waitress was back in record time. Legend shocked everyone around her when she pulled out a hundred-dollar bill and dropped it on the tray. The waitress stepped in and kissed her as a thank you. Legend slid her hand around her waist and pulled her closer, deepening the kiss, eliciting howls and cheers from the group. The waitress set aside her tray and slid her hands up around Legend's neck, pressing her body close.

Afterward, Legend turned to the table and handed out the shots.

"Nicely done," Remington said.

"Semper fi," Legend said seriously, holding her glass up.

"Semper fi!" Kai and Remington repeated vehemently.

Everyone around the table nodded, holding their glasses up as well.

Later, Kai, Remington, and Legend were sitting outside on the patio, smoking.

"So you're trying to show people what it was really like," Remington said.

"I want people to know what it did to rip people apart," Legend said.

Remington nodded. "It was far from easy."

"But you made it past Don't Ask, Don't Tell—I didn't," Legend said. "DADT ended my career."

Kai and Remington nodded.

"It would have ended mine too," Kai said. "Especially since the affair I did have was with my married CO."

"Holy shit!" Legend exclaimed.

Kai laughed.

"Speaking of which," Remington said, "Kathy been around lately?"

"Not since she saw me with Fin here last time. But I'm sure I haven't seen the last of her."

"Kathy?" Legend asked.

"The CO," Remington said.

"Oh…" Legend's eyes widened. "She's still after you?"

Kai rolled her eyes, nodding.

"Speaking of women," Remington said, grinning, "I hear you sleep with most of your leading ladies… gay or straight. Any truth to that?"

Legend grinned, her light eyes sparkling mischievously. "There've been a few," she said. "And no, they weren't all gay to start with."

"Nice…" Kai said, chuckling.

"So how many toasters do you have?" Remington asked.

Legend laughed, shaking her head. "Lost count a long time ago."

"Seriously, though," Kai said, giving Legend a pointed look. "I think what you're doing is really brave, and I really hope you get the truth out there."

"That's my plan," Legend said.

Remington and Kai both nodded.

"Now, you two make sure you're safe over there, and come home to those two incredibly beautiful women," Legend said.

"Oorah," Remington said.

"Oorah," Kai repeated.

"Oorah," Legend added.

Later that night, on the way back from the party, Riley glanced over at Legend. "You are okay to drive, aren't you?" she asked.

Legend nodded. "I'm good, I promise."

"Did you have a good time?"

"I did. They're a pretty cool group... the hard-stare party of cops notwithstanding," she added with a grin.

"No one hassled you, did they?"

"No," Legend said, shaking her head. "But I'd bet that was because I'm not high tonight."

Riley grimaced. She didn't like how often Legend stated that she wasn't high "tonight"—it indicated that there were other times. She wasn't sure how many other times it implied, and that worried her.

That night after the party, Wynter and Remington were at home. Remington was to report the day after next. Wynter had been quiet since the morning Remington had found out she was being deployed. She was working on dealing with the idea that Remington was going to be gone. The orders they'd received had said one to two months. The fact that she wasn't being sent back to the Middle East was good, but being deployed to an area that was seismically unstable wasn't necessarily better.

As they went to bed that night, Wynter held on to Remington with all of her might. Remington knew Wynter was struggling with her deployment, and she knew it was something she needed to work out for herself. She held Wynter to her, kissing her temple.

"I love you," Remington said. "And when I get back I'm going to marry you, so you better be working on those plans while I'm gone."

"So this is how you're getting out of having to do the planning?" Wynter asked.

"Modi li, you figured me out."

"Not as slick as you think you are, Marine," Wynter said, smiling now.

"Oh, I'm plenty slick."

"I don't know… Let's find out," Wynter said, sliding her hand down Remington's stomach.

They were making love minutes later, reminding each other why they were so good together. In the end they made love most of the night, never able to truly get enough of each other. It had been that way from the beginning, and it hadn't changed in the year they'd been together.

Early the next morning, regardless of a complete lack of sleep,

Wynter lay in Remington's arms, staring up at the amazing woman she was engaged to marry.

"Remi, I'm sorry," she said softly.

"Pou kisa?" Remington asked, her fatigue making her slip into her usual Creole. "Sorry for what, babe?"

"For making this so hard on you."

"You didn't make it hard, Wyn. It is hard—leaving people you love always is."

"But my freak-out didn't help."

Remington gazed back at Wynter, reaching up to touch her cheek. "You love me—loving me means you're going to worry," she said. "And I'm sorry for that. But knowing I'm coming home to you will make it worth it to me."

"Well, from here on out, I'm going to become the Marine wife I need to be."

Remington grinned. "You are, huh?"

"Yes." Wynter nodded firmly. "Today we're going to get you ready to go. And tomorrow I'm going to kiss you goodbye and spend time planning our wedding for when you come home."

"You might want to do some work on your new album, too, or BJ might fire you," Remington said.

"Oh, I plan on it," Wynter said with a sparkle in her eyes.

"Bon bondye…" Remington breathed—*Good God* in Creole, which Wynter understood.

"What?" Wynter asked, grinning.

"Why do I think the direction of your new album just changed?"

"Because it did."

"BJ'll be thrilled…"

Wynter winked. "He will when I win a Grammy with it."

Meanwhile, in the Temple/Taylor household, Kai was getting her gear together while Finley sat watching. She'd always been fascinated by the Marine side of Kai. It still scared her to have her being deployed. Like Wynter, she wasn't completely comforted by the idea that it wouldn't be people shooting at them, but rather Mother Nature herself being the danger. Mother Nature was even less predictable than people.

When Kai had finished packing her duffle, she came to lie down next to Finley, pulling her into her arms.

"You okay?" Kai asked, noting that Finley had been quiet.

"I'm getting there," Finley said, smiling softly. "I guess I never really thought you'd get deployed."

Kai nodded. "Unfortunately, because of the resources the dogs offer, my unit gets deployed more often than most."

"That wasn't in the brochure when I signed up," Finley said sourly.

Kai grinned. "Sorry."

"Mmhmm…" Finley murmured, resting her head against the hollow of Kai's shoulder.

"I was thinking…" Kai said, hesitant to bring it up, but feeling like it was important enough to risk it.

Finley glanced up at her, seeing the serious look on her face.

"What?"

Kai turned on her side, facing Finley. "If we were married and something happened…" she began.

"No," Finley said, shaking her head.

"Fin, listen…"

"No, Kai. No," Finley said vehemently, sitting up. "We're not going to talk about this."

Kai sat up as well, taking Finley's face in her hands. "If we're not married, there's no guarantees what would happen if—"

"No!" Finley yelled, tears in her eyes.

"Fin, we have to be realistic here."

"Fuck realistic, Kai. Nothing is going to happen, and you're coming back to me. Promise me that."

"I can't do that," Kai said, shaking her head sadly.

"Why?"

"Because by doing that I'm tempting Fate to defy me," Kai said. "And I won't do that."

Finley's lips trembled. She knew Kai had a very different philosophy about things, on top of the Marine superstitions, such as not talking about someone dying.

"Wait, why are you allowed to talk about you dying, but I can't?" she asked.

Kai stared back at her, her lips twitching. "It's different."

"How?"

"Because you saying it wishes me bad luck."

"But you saying it isn't a self-fulfilling prophecy?" Finley countered.

Kai pursed her lips. "I couldn't tell you."

"Then if I don't get to talk about it, neither do you," Finley said, folding her arms.

Kai nodded, acquiescing to her concerns. She later contacted her lawyers, making necessary changes to her will to include Finley, and altered her wishes with regard to her estate and Cassiana's custody, which she would pass to Finley, along with the house, cars, and all of her financial holdings, which were fairly substantial. She made sure that a letter containing the changes would arrive at the house in the event of her death. It was imperative to her that Finley be taken care of, as well as Cassiana.

That night, when they went to bed, Kai made love to Finley, telling her over and over with her body how much she loved her. The next morning she got up and put on her battle dress uniform, complete with her rank and insignia. When she walked out into the kitchen, where Cassiana and Finley were sitting, Finley felt her heart flutter. Kai made an extremely handsome, sexy Marine. She watched as Kai set her cover on the counter and poured herself coffee.

"What time do you pick up Remi?" Finley asked, moving over to Kai and leaning against the counter.

Kai glanced at her watch. "About forty-five minutes."

"And you're reporting to Pendleton?"

"Yep," Kai said, leaning down to kiss her softly.

Finley slid her hands up around Kai's neck. "You look damned handsome."

"Thank you." Kai grinned, her dark eyes shining.

"I remember the last time I saw you in this uniform."

"Yeah, I had a few more bruises."

"Yes, you did, but you still looked sexy then too."

"I love you," Kai said, knowing that Finley was doing her best to be brave.

Finley bit her lower lip, tears glazing her eyes suddenly. "I love you."

"Hey, do me a favor," Kai said, setting her coffee down and reaching up to her BDU shirt pocket.

"What?"

"When I get back," Kai said, pulling something out of her pocket, "marry me, will ya?"

Finley blinked as she saw the ring Kai was holding in front of her.

"Oh my God!" Cassiana exclaimed from behind them.

"Kai…" Finley breathed, her brandy-colored eyes wide as she stared up at Kai.

"I love you, and I want to know that when I come home you'll be here waiting for me, with this on," Kai said, sliding the band onto Finley's left ring finger.

"Not waiting for an answer, are you?" Finley asked.

"Nope," Kai said. "I've learned that giving you options isn't a good idea," she added, winking.

Finley laughed, looking down at the ring. It was incredibly beautiful, with a swirl of gold that looked similar to that of a wave, culminating in two round-cut diamonds.

"Kai, this is beautiful," she said, glancing up. "Is it that Irish designer?" she asked, thinking that it looked similar to one of the rings that Kai wore.

"Yes, Sheila Fleet."

"So you had to order this…"

"About three months ago."

"And you've had it this whole time."

"Waiting for the right time."

"Deploying is the right time?"

"To prove to you that I'm coming home."

Finley reached up to hug Kai. "I love you," she whispered against her neck.

"So that's a yes?" Kai asked, grinning.

"Of course it's a yes. You knew that."

"Well, I hoped I did, yeah."

Finley stepped back, taking Kai's face in her hands. "I will be here waiting for you when you come home. And I will marry you after you get back."

"Then I have a reason to come back," Kai said. "Oh yeah, and you too," she said, winking at Cassiana.

"Oh, sure," Cassiana said, rolling her eyes.

Before Kai left, she held Finley for a long moment. "I'll call you when we get there. I love you."

Cassiana and Finley stood in the garage and watched Kai drive away.

Later, Finley was lying on their bed, with Chip on one side of her and Digger on the other, when Cassiana knocked softly on the door.

"Come on in," Finley called.

Cassiana walked into the room and saw the tears on Finley's cheeks. Without a word, she shoved Chip aside and lay down with her back against Finley's side. Finley turned over, putting her arm around Cassiana's waist.

"She'll be okay, you know," Cassiana said.

Finley smiled sadly. "I'm supposed to comfort you, ya know," she said softly.

Cassiana chuckled. "Okay, comfort away."

"I already miss her."

"Me too."

Wynter was completely floored when Remington walked down the stairs wearing her BDUs. Remington had deferred a number of her weekends in the reserves because of her job protecting Wynter. This was the first time Wynter had seen her in uniform.

"Oh, bondye…" Wynter breathed, her blue eyes sparkling, having picked up the habit from Remington.

Remington grinned, loving that Wynter not only spoke her native language, but spoke it with a perfect accent. It was one of the many things she loved about the passionate rock star.

"I take it you like the uniform?" Remington asked unnecessarily.

"You take it right," Wynter said, smiling widely. "You look very... hot."

Remington made a grunting noise as she reached up, touching her hair. Wynter had finally had the pleasure the day before of seeing what Remington's hair looked like out of the customary cornrows. She'd had them redone minus the red tipping they usually had; she knew if she showed up to base with the red tips, she'd never hear the end of it from her CO. Her hair, now back to its original dark brown, seemed odd to her. She'd had it cut three inches shorter, since it had grown a great deal over the last year. It still felt strange.

"Your hair is fine, babe," Wynter said, smiling. "Although I was all for leaving it completely out..."

"Ou se fou," Remington said, telling Wynter she was crazy. "I wouldn't have time to do a damned thing if I had to mess with all of this every day."

Wynter pressed her lips together, her blue eyes sparkling. "Okay, babe."

Remington knew she was being placated. Instead of answering, she poured herself a cup of coffee.

"When will Kai be here?" Wynter asked.

Remington looked at her watch. "Twenty minutes."

"Memphis and Kieran will be here any minute."

"You need to be strong for her."

"I know," Wynter said. "I will, I promise. I'll make sure she's okay."

Memphis had formed a major attachment to Remington over

the last year and a half. Remington was like a mother to her, and it was killing Memphis that she was being deployed. Kieran had told Wynter that Memphis was throwing up regularly again and sleeping a lot, which meant she was slipping into a depression. Kieran was watching Memphis closely, and they'd talked to Finley about her as well. Finley was talking to Savanna about prescribing an anti-depressant. Everyone was coming together to help.

The doorbell rang, and Wynter went to get it. Memphis walked in, hugging Wynter, looking morose. As Kieran hugged Wynter, Memphis went into the kitchen and straight over to Remington, who had just enough time to put her coffee down before Memphis embraced her. Remington held the smaller girl, kissing the top of her head repeatedly, her hand on the back of Memphis' head.

When Memphis stepped back, she put out her hand. Remington grinned as she pulled out her phone, handing it over. Memphis walked over to the kitchen table, pulled out her laptop, and plugged in the phone.

"New playlist?" Remington asked.

"Yep," Memphis said. "And you'll need to share with Kai too."

"You got it," Remington said, smiling indulgently, even as she and Wynter exchanged a look.

Memphis was forever putting new music on everyone's phones. She especially enjoyed doing so for Remington. It was her way of loving people; music was Memphis' life and her love, next to Kieran. Kieran gave Remington a hug.

"Take good care of her while I'm gone, huh?" Remington said softly.

"I will, I promise," Kieran said, her English accent clear.

All too quickly, it was time for Remington to go; Kai had just pulled up outside in her green Mercedes.

"Does she always have to be on time?" Wynter asked jokingly.

Remington grinned. "It's a Marine thing."

She hugged each of them, kissing Wynter over and over, then hugged Memphis one more time.

"You take care of yourself, little one," she said.

"I will," Memphis said, tears slipping down her cheek. "You come back safe."

"I will," Remington said. "I promise."

Memphis nodded as she stepped back.

Remington walked out to the car. Kai popped the trunk, and Remington put her duffel in before getting inside, waving to the three women standing outside the house.

"Your house looks like mine did this morning," Kai said as she pulled out of the driveway.

"Yeah, this sucks."

"It does, yeah."

Remington reached over, unplugging Kai's iPhone and plugging hers in instead.

"Memphis give us a playlist?" Kai asked.

"Of course."

The first song that came on was by Linkin Park, "Hands Held High." It was basically a protest about the war. One of the lines said, "When the rich wage war, it's the poor who die."

"Think she has an opinion about the military right now?" Kai asked, grinning, as she accelerated onto the freeway toward southern California.

Remington smiled back. "Ya think?"

Chapter 3

It was another two weeks before Legend saw Georgette again. She'd been out with her unit for all that time and had just gotten back to the barracks after a long, hot shower. She was lying in her bunk, her eyes closed, when Georgette walked in.

She went to the side of the bed, scanning Legend's face. She'd thought about her so often in the last two weeks. At first she had been sure that Legend was avoiding her, but by carefully checking, she'd found out that she had instead been on an extended mission with her unit. Still, she had no idea where things stood between them.

She sat down on Legend's bunk, reaching out to touch Legend's arm. Legend jumped; she'd been dead asleep. Her eyes flew open.

"I missed you," Georgette said.

"Ya just scared the shit out of me," Legend said sharply.

"Sorry, I just... I thought you were avoiding me, and I didn't want to give you the chance."

Legend narrowed her eyes. "I've been back all of about an hour. I needed a shower and some shut-eye."

Georgette blinked a couple of times, her blue eyes reflecting her shock at Legend's tone.

Legend did her best to keep her expression stern. She needed Georgette to back off; it was better for both of them if they weren't around each other anymore.

Georgette reached out, touching Legend's face, searching her eyes.

Legend needed to get away from that look, from Georgette's touch. She sat up, putting her head back against the wall above her bunk, as far away from Georgette as she could get.

Instead of being dissuaded, however, Georgette moved closer, leaning her head against Legend's chest, curling her hand around the material of Legend's tank top. Legend closed her eyes. She felt a tremor run through her body at the feel of Georgette against her. Her arm automatically went around her shoulders before she could stop it. Georgette's reaction was to look up at Legend, surprising her by reaching up and putting her hand around Legend's neck. It was far too easy to lower her head and kiss her.

When their lips met, there was no turning back. Georgette pressed closer, moaning softly against Legend's lips. It was Legend's undoing. Her arm around Georgette's shoulders pulled the other woman over her own body, her other hand coming up to pull Georgette up to her face. She deepened the kiss and ran her hands over Georgette's uniform, pulling her shirt out of her pants, sliding her hand over Georgette's skin. Georgette shuddered and pressed her body against Legend's, moving rhythmically. Legend guided her body, pressing it against her in the right places, and before long they were both coming, gasping and moaning as they grasped at each other.

"Jesus, this is crazy. We can't be here," Legend said as she calmed her breathing.

"I locked the door to the barracks on my way in," Georgette said.

"Okay, even that is dangerous."

"If someone tries the door, you just open it and say it must have locked accidentally," Georgette said reasonably.

71

Legend shook her head. "You don't get it, George. Anything I do is suspect, and having you in here when I 'accidentally' locked the door will set them on an investigation of both of us."

Georgette stared back at her, shocked.

"I already push the boundaries," Legend said. "With my look, I'm always suspect. If they see that I'm around you too much, they're going to start watching more carefully. So if we're going to do this, you gotta be careful. When we see each other, you can't look... like that," she said, nodding at Georgette, seeing the way she was staring intently into her eyes.

"No one is here," Georgette said.

"I know, but I'm saying you have to be careful."

"Okay."

"You can't treat me any different out there," Legend said, gesturing to the outside.

"Can you stop telling me what I can't do for a minute?" Georgette asked, her blue eyes sparkling.

Legend couldn't help but grin. The look Georgette was giving her was far too appealing. She leaned in, kissing her again, reveling in the feel of being this close to her. She knew it was dangerous, and she knew they'd have to be ultra-careful, but she didn't care at that moment. Pulling Georgette close, mindful that the doors were locked, she pulled Georgette's shirt off. Georgette responded by sitting up long enough to take off the rest of her clothes, which gave Legend the time to do the same. When their bodies met, there was no more discussion of what was okay and what wasn't. They made love, enjoying each other thoroughly, and lay together afterward, breathing heavily; Georgette lay *half over Legend, exactly the way Legend wanted it.*

"I never imagined this," *Georgette said, her tone wondrous.*

"Most girls don't grow up dreaming about lesbian sex, babe," *Legend said mildly.*

"Is that what I am? A lesbian?"

"Not necessarily." *Legend shrugged.* "It could just be that you're far from home and need something…"

"What would make me a lesbian?"

Legend grinned. "Well, there's no pill to take, if that's what you're looking for…"

Georgette poked Legend in the ribs with a fingernail, making her jump and laugh.

"I mean, how would I know if I am?" *Georgette asked.*

Legend shook her head. "I don't know…"

"How did you know?"

"When I could only have close relationships with women, and being with men seemed unnatural to me."

Georgette nodded, looking pensive. "Would being in love with you count?" *she asked after a few moments.*

Legend's mouth fell open, her eyes widening in surprise. Then she started to shake her head, wanting to deny what Georgette was saying.

"You've been all I could think about for the last two weeks, Legend," *Georgette said.* "It broke my heart when you told me to leave before. I love you. I don't know how it happened, but I love you."

Legend grimaced, but nodded, knowing this was only going to make things harder.

73

Riley walked up to Legend's bedroom door, thinking she was forever having to wake this woman up but happy that Legend was apparently sleeping. Tula had gotten so used to Riley by this point that she merely pointed upstairs when she arrived. Walking into the bedroom, Riley saw Legend lying on the bed in what was apparently common apparel for her—faded, tattered jeans and a tank top; today's was white, stark against her tanned skin.

"Legend?" Riley said softly.

Legend stirred right away, turning her head and grinning.

"I was going to stay awake this time," she muttered.

"Sure, sure," Riley said, waving her hand airily. "It's just a ploy to get me into your bedroom, I know that."

Legend chuckled, turning over on her side and patting the bed next to her.

"See what I'm sayin'?" Riley said even as she walked around the bed, pulling the curtains open slightly to let in some light.

"Jovina give you the rewrites?" Legend asked.

"Yes," Riley said, and started to hand them to Legend.

Legend shook her head. "Read it to me," she said tiredly.

"Okay." It was clear that Legend was in no condition to read the pages at that point. "This is the scene where Lizette and Georgia make love for the first time," she said, and saw an immediate flicker of pain across Legend's face.

"Go ahead," Legend said, looking like she was steeling herself.

"We can wait…"

"I need to know it's right," Legend said, pulling a pillow over to hold it under her chin as she stared up at Riley. Her eyes looked gold in the sunlight coming through the windows.

Riley began reading the scene as written in the screenplay, including the stage directions.

"Georgia, you were avoiding me—"

Legend held up her hand, shaking her head. "No, change that to 'I thought you were avoiding me.' She knew I wasn't."

Riley stared back at Legend for a long moment. She knew a lot of the movie was straight from how things had actually happened; sometimes she realized how closely, like at that moment. She nodded, pulling out a pen and a highlighter, and made the correction.

"You really shouldn't have to do this," Legend said, not for the first time since they'd been working together. "It's really not your job."

"Does anyone else know how close this is to your life?"

Legend looked pensive, then shook her head.

"Do you want people to know?"

"No," Legend said immediately.

"Well, that's why I'm doing this with you instead."

Legend smiled softly. "Guess I got more than I bargained for when I put you in the part, huh? Gonna have to increase your cut of the profits, if there are any."

"There will be," Riley said confidently.

"Pretty sure about that?" Legend asked, trying to ignore the warmth that spread through her heart at the thought.

"Damned sure, actually," Riley said. "Now, can we finish reading through this scene?" she asked wryly.

Legend smiled, licking her lips in amusement. "Sure, do you want to run through the *entire* scene?" she asked, her look pointed as she waggled her eyebrows suggestively.

"You are so bad..." Riley said, shaking her head. "No wonder you've managed to seduce all of your leading ladies."

"Not all of them," Legend said with an unapologetic grin.

"No? How many of them haven't you seduced? Because I'm betting it's the shorter list."

"Allexxiss Ramsey-Sparks."

"And?"

"That's the list," Legend said, her eyes sparkling mischievously.

"You're that good?"

"Wanna find out?" Legend asked, sitting up.

"No," Riley said, holding her hand up. "We have work to do."

Legend put her tongue between her lips, grinning evilly. "Fine!" she said, leaning back against the headboard of her bed. "Read me the next lines."

They finished going through the lines, and Riley glanced at Legend. "Can I ask you a question?"

"Yeah."

"You obviously didn't want her to decide she was a lesbian. Why?"

Legend looked thoughtful for a long moment.

"Being a lesbian is one thing, Ri. Being a lesbian in the Marines is a whole other thing. You aren't free to be yourself—you aren't free to be anything they haven't authorized you to be. If she decided she was a lesbian, I knew she'd suddenly know the heartache of it. I didn't want that for her."

"You loved her already at that point, didn't you?"

Legend curled her lips in derision. "Yeah, I did, and it was bound to doom us both."

"It was that serious? Don't Ask, Don't Tell?"

"You know, the funny thing is, people actually think DADT made it easier on gays, 'cause they couldn't ask, right? Well, that's the thing. They didn't ask—they accused. More gays were put out of the military under DADT than any other policy they ever had before that. And worse still, more women were put out under DADT."

"Why?" Riley asked.

Legend gave a short, mirthless laugh. "Because the military doesn't really have much use for us women anyway. If we're not going to be useful as sex toys, there's really no point in us being there, right?"

Riley blinked a couple of times, surprised, but Legend had the experience of living through it, so she knew better than she did. "That's really awful."

"That's the US military during DADT," Legend said. "At least, in my experience."

Riley nodded, understanding a little better why Legend was dedicated to telling this story. She still had no idea what had happened between her and Georgia, because Legend hadn't given anyone that part of the script yet. She was planning to give them sections as they needed them. It was the best way to keep any plot twists from leaking, and it was the way Legend worked on all of her films.

"Was her name really Georgia?" Riley asked.

"Georgette," Legend said, her smile soft.

Riley nodded. "Well, I'm going to get out of here, and maybe you can get some more sleep," she said, getting up.

"You're sure you don't want to just run through the scene..." Legend asked, her eyes sparkling again.

"I'm sure," Riley said, giving her a narrowed look.

Legend laughed. "Can't blame a girl for tryin'."

"I can, actually," Riley said, her hands on her hips.

"Ohh..." Legend said, smiling impudently.

"How is she doing?" Wynter asked Kieran as she looked out onto her patio, where Memphis sat, drinking a beer and smoking.

She'd invited them to dinner the night after Kai and Remington left, wanting to make sure Memphis was okay.

Kieran grimaced. "I'm not sure that working on this movie with Legend Azaria at this point in time is a good idea..."

"Why do you say that?" Wynter asked, aware that Memphis was excited at the prospect of learning a new area of sound production.

"Can you hear that music she's listening to? It's awful," Kieran said, shuddering as she hugged herself. "It's so dark."

"What is it?" Wynter asked, trying to hear the music that was playing on Memphis' phone.

"It's called *The Heroin Diaries*. Apparently it's what Legend is listening to now to get into the feel of the movie. So she's got Memphis listening it."

"Okay, but you know Memphis—she loves new areas of music."

"I don't like it," Kieran said. "It's all about drug use and dying. It's not what she needs to be thinking about right now."

Wynter nodded and walked outside, wanting to talk to Memphis herself. She'd already noted that Memphis was wearing the black, red, and gray Tapout hoodie that Remington often wore; she had lent it to Memphis the night before she'd left. Wynter had been certain Remington had meant for Memphis to have it while she was gone, to keep her close. That was the way Remington was, always protecting the people she loved, even from thousands of miles away. Wynter loved that about her.

"How are you doing?" Wynter asked as she sat across from Memphis.

Memphis nodded, looking like she was trying to be brave.

"What's this?" Wynter gestured to Memphis' phone.

Memphis gave her a narrowed look, telling her that she knew damned well that Kieran had already told her.

"Okay, okay," Wynter said, holding up her hands in surrender. "I know what it is. I just want to make sure you're okay."

"I don't do heroin, Wyn."

"I know that," Wynter said. "But your mental state is what I'm worried about."

"I checked in with Savanna."

"What did she say?"

"She says I'm having a depressive episode." Memphis shrugged. "Like Cody does, only not as bad."

Wynter nodded. "And what does she want to do about that?"

Memphis looked pensive, chewing on the inside of her cheek. "She wants to put me on meds."

Wynter tilted her head, sensing Memphis' reluctance. "And?"

Memphis shook her head. "I don't wanna do it."

"Why?"

"That shit…" Memphis said pensively. "It messes with the creative… You know?"

Wynter nodded, knowing exactly what Memphis meant, but she wasn't sure that it was safe for her not to take medication.

"You know what I don't get," Memphis said, picking at a thread on the hoodie. "Why did they call up the infantry?" she asked, her tone indicating her annoyance with the military at that point.

"I actually asked Remi that," Wynter said. "She said that whenever other units get called up, they call up an infantry unit to go too. The infantry basically protects the back of the other units, plus does crowd control and overall protection of the affected areas."

"To keep them from looting and stuff?"

Wynter nodded. "Yeah."

"So, as usual, Remi's protecting someone else with her life," Memphis said, her expression sad, but proud too.

"That's what our girl does, right?" Wynter said, smiling softly.

"Yeah."

They were both quiet for a long moment, then Wynter looked

over at Memphis.

"Will you promise me something?" she said.

"What?"

"That you'll stay in touch with Savanna, or even with Cody…"

Memphis gazed back at Wynter, her blue eyes reflecting amusement. "Remi told you to take care of me, didn't she?"

"Remi loves you and wants to make sure you're okay," Wynter said. "But I love you too, and I want to know you're okay too."

Memphis nodded. "Okay, I'll talk to Cody. I promise."

"Okay."

Later that night, they got a call from Remington, who regaled them with their flight and the accommodations, which were at best lousy.

"I'm thinking I'll sleep in Kai's office—it's bigger than the room we're sharing," Remington said, chuckling.

"How are things there?" Wynter asked.

"A little bit chaotic. But they've got us assigned to a section of town, so hopefully when we get there we'll be able to set up some decent parameters of operation."

They talked for a while longer, but it was apparent that Remington was tired; her accent was becoming more prevalent, and she was using more and more Creole without even realizing it, a sure sign of fatigue.

"Okay, babe, we're going to let you go. You get some rest, okay?" Wynter said, exchanging a look with Memphis, who nodded emphatically.

"Okay," Remington said. "I love you."

"I love you, Wynter said.

"Memphis?" Remington queried.

"Yeah, Remi?"

"Take care of my girl for me, huh?" Remington said, a smile in her voice.

Memphis smiled. "You got it. Love you."

"Love you too, little one."

They hung up. Wynter went to bed that night feeling bereft, and knowing it was going to be the longest month to two months of her life. She hadn't realized how used to having Remington right there with her she'd gotten until she suddenly wasn't there. It left a hole in her life a mile long, and she missed her like crazy.

Kai had called Finley and Cassiana that same evening. She sounded exhausted, but Finley was happy to hear her voice regardless. They talked about the room she and Remington were sharing, and how Kai had had the same idea of sleeping in her office.

"You have an office?" Finley asked, surprised.

"Yeah, at the Italian consulate, because at this point I'm one of the highest-ranking officers on this operation."

"Wow," Finley said. "My girl's in charge…" She trailed off suggestively.

"Don't get too excited," Kai said, a grin in her voice. "It probably won't last. I'm sure we'll end up with at least one general here."

"Not likely to be your dad, is it?"

"Bite your tongue," Kai said, her voice low. "Seriously, though, it's not likely they'd send a four-star here. Probably just a brigadier."

"A one-star," Cassiana explained to Finley.

"Oh," Finley said, nodding.

They hung up not too much later, because Finley could tell that Kai was tired. Kai promised to email her as often as possible to let her know what was going on.

"I love you," Finley said. "Please just stay safe over there."

"Roger that," Kai said tiredly. "I love you both."

Cassiana smiled. "Love you too, KaiMarou."

"Still a damned Pokémon character…" Kai muttered, which had both Finley and Cassiana laughing.

"You call me when you get there," Cat said to Jovina as everyone grouped at the airport.

"I will," Jovina said, reaching up to kiss her. "You're not going to work yourself into the ground while I'm gone, are you?"

"I'll try not to," Cat said, grinning.

"That isn't very reassuring, my love," Jovina said, narrowing her gold eyes.

"I love you, Jovi," Cat said, leaning in to kiss her gain.

Jovina sighed. "You know it makes me melt when you call me that, which is why you do it."

Cat grinned unrepentantly. "Tell me you love me, Jovi," she whispered against her lips.

"I love you," Jovina said, smiling. "And I will miss you like crazy."

"I'll miss you too, babe. You be… careful over there."

Jovina looked back at Catalina for a long moment. "I know what you're worried about," she said softly. "And you don't need to worry. I'm in love with a narc—I'm not stupid enough to get into drugs again. I know I'd lose you then."

Catalina drew Jovina into her arms, hugging her, not wanting to say anything but knowing Jovina was right; she couldn't and wouldn't handle Jovina doing drugs again. They had a history where that was concerned, and it wasn't something Cat would ever compromise on.

Everyone else in the group said their goodbyes to their loved ones. The flashiest arrival was Talon Valois, who turned up in a red Ferrari driven by what had to be a porn star. The woman practically gave the actress a tonsillectomy in front of the entire cast and crew. Talon walked up to the group, her grin roguish; it was certainly an entrance.

Legend was already on the plane in first class when everyone boarded; she'd reserved the whole section as well as all of the business-class seats so that everyone would be comfortable. Riley was sitting with Legend, and Talon and Jovina ended up right behind them. Other cast members took up seats, glancing at their enigmatic director. Everyone had been hand-selected by Legend Azaria, but some of them were still a bit gun-shy about the director they'd heard was extremely talented but tough.

It was an eleven-hour flight to Paris, and from there another three hours to Rabat, Morocco, where they'd be filming.

"Please tell me you're going to try to sleep some of this flight," Riley said softly to Legend, who was already making notes in her ever-present notebook.

Riley had learned early on that Legend always carried a leather-bound notebook with her, which she used to make notes about whatever project she was working on. It had pictures stuffed into it, maps, plans, drawings, and tons of notes. She considered it her bible for the duration of a film, from development to pre-production, to production and post-production.

"Uh… yeah… not likely," Legend said, grinning.

"You haven't slept for the last three days…"

"I slept for like an hour yesterday," Legend pointed out as she reached up to scratch her head.

Riley saw that Legend's hand was shaking, so she reached over, taking it and squeezing it gently. Legend nodded, acknowledging what Riley was trying to do.

"Not worried the rumors will start about an affair between us already?" Legend asked, holding their clasped hands up slightly.

"Don't care about that," Riley said. "More worried about any other rumors."

Legend licked her lips, nodding. "I'll try to get some sleep too, okay?"

"Yes, please," Riley said softly.

Legend squeezed her hand gently before letting it go to continue her notes. She was also reviewing the script, making changes and handing them back to Jovina as she did. Jovina had her laptop out and was working on making Legend's corrections.

"So you get a working flight, huh?" Talon asked.

Jovina smiled. "Unless you'd like to have no lines to say when we get there."

"I could just make stuff up," Talon said, stretching her long, jean-clad legs out in front of her.

"Not anything Legend would allow you to say, I'm sure," Jovina said, glancing at the very attractive actress.

She'd heard a lot about Talon Valois, not the least of which was that she was a womanizer to the nth degree. Jovina had seen a number of Talon's movies, and the woman was indeed a chameleon. Her previous movie, she'd played a very sexy FBI agent on the hunt for a serial killer, with long hair and full makeup. For this film, her face was completely makeup free, and her long black hair had been cropped short to mimic a Marine haircut; it was very butch.

Jovina caught the sparkle of interest in Talon's green eyes and laughed softly, shaking her head.

"What?" Talon asked, staring back at her.

"You're not considering coming on to me, are you?"

Talon gazed at the hot Latina. As a matter of fact, she had been, and her expression reflected that fact.

"I'll save you some time," Jovina said, smiling. "I'm dating a very beautiful narcotics cop who wears a very nasty-looking gun on her hip daily and carries a badge."

"And it's working?" Talon asked, her eyes widening slightly.

"I'm in love with her, yes."

Talon smiled widely. "Got respect for that," she said, inclining her head. "I'm sure your girl is used to other women coming on to you."

"That doesn't make her less dangerous to piss off," Jovina said, her gold eyes sparkling as she batted her eyelashes sweetly.

"Message received," Talon said, holding up her hands in surrender. "Hopefully we can still be friends."

"I think that might be possible."

"Good," Talon said, smiling.

The flight proceeded uneventfully, and sixteen hours later they arrived at their location for the shoot. Sets had been built, and it looked like a minor military base. A sort of barracks had been set up for the crew members. The stars and Legend had their own small rooms with their own private bathrooms. Others, like Jovina and the assistant director and Tula, were put in groups of two or three.

Legend called everyone to order before letting them go to their rooms.

"Everyone settle in and get some sleep. We're starting bright and early tomorrow at five a.m.—welcome to being Marines," she said, winking at them all with a grin on her lips. "Riley and Talon, I'll need you two in makeup by four thirty."

Both Riley and Talon nodded.

"Okay, grab some dinner, settle in, and we'll see you all in the morning!" Legend stepped down off the table she'd been standing on.

"And that means you too, right?" Riley said, next to her immediately.

"Which part?"

"Oh, the eating and sleeping, since you didn't sleep on the plane at all…"

"Yes, dear," Legend said, rolling her eyes.

"Don't sass me," Riley said, putting her hands on her hips.

Legend laughed softly, shaking her head. "You do realize you're only six years older than me, right?"

"Sometimes it seems like decades," Riley said chidingly.

She wound her arm around Legend's and started walking her toward the building that had been designated as the chow hall.

"Not gonna take any chances?" Legend asked.

"Nope," Riley said. "You also didn't touch the food the ever-helpful flight attendant brought you while trying to flirt you right out of those jeans."

"Now that sounds like jealousy…" Legend said, grinning mischievously.

"No, that sounds like fact. And a fact you didn't even notice, which says you're hyper-focusing and not taking care of yourself."

"So you're gonna take care of me?" Legend asked pointedly.

"Oh, I'm sure I'm not the first to try," Riley said, her voice indicating her lack of hope that it would work.

"Nope," Legend said simply.

"Won't stop me from trying, just like I'd try to take care of my daughter if she was as stubborn as you and didn't have Kai for that now."

"How is Kai? Have they heard from her and Remi?" Legend asked as they entered the hall.

"Yes, they're fine," Riley said. "They're apparently in fairly cramped quarters, but otherwise adjusting like good Marines."

"Oorah," Legend said, grinning.

Riley smiled. "Indeed."

She managed to get Legend to eat a sandwich and then prodded her to go to her own accommodations and get some sleep. At the door to Legend's bungalow, Riley gave her a pointed look.

"You're going to try to sleep, right?"

Legend stared back at her for a long moment, her expression pointedly blank.

"Legend..." Riley began.

"Okay, okay, Uncle," Legend said, rolling her eyes. "Yeah, okay, I'll try."

Riley nodded, not feeling very confident about what Legend was saying, but realizing she needed to back off before she made her mad.

"Thank you," she said softly. "I'll see you in the morning."

Legend nodded, turning to go into her bungalow. Inside, she looked around. Her bags were set to the side, and Tula had obviously unpacked for her. Her overnight bag was on the bed, untouched; Tula knew better than to unpack that particular one. She pulled out her notebook, her iPod and headphones, cigarettes, lighter, and a couple of bottles of pills. She opened the nightstand drawer and dropped the bottles in, her lips twitching as she closed the drawer again.

She took a shower, put on sweatpants and a tank top, and lay down on the bed, plugging her headphones into her ears and finding the song she'd been thinking about. Hitting play on the iPod, she closed her eyes and let the music pump through her head. The words drummed right into her mind. The lyrics talked about how basically everyone had highs and lows, but added the ominous comments that people got used and sold. It spoke volumes about her state of mind.

Legend knew she was pushing things right now. She knew she was walking an edge she shouldn't be on, but she couldn't stop. She had to see this through. Georgette deserved it; she honestly didn't care if it killed her in the end.

She didn't sleep, couldn't sleep—there was too much running through her head. Getting up, she reached into the drawer and found the green bottle. She took out a pill and popped it into her mouth. She ended up getting coffee from the chow hall at two in the morning, sitting at one of the tables, music pumping through her head as she wrote endlessly in her notebook. When people started waking up and wandering in to get coffee, they found her there.

Filming started that day. They worked in progression with the story, a rarity in film making, but it was the way Legend needed to work on this particular story. She needed things to progress the way they had. The first day was spent getting characters established and doing some read throughs to ensure that Talon and Riley were jibing in terms of chemistry. Fortunately, Riley's many years working in movies gave her the ability to work with anyone. Talon, as talented as she was, having adored Riley Taylor since she'd been a teenager, was thrilled to get a chance to work with the Academy Award–winning actress. She commented a number of times that Riley hadn't aged a day since she'd been in Hollywood.

"That would make me five, honey," Riley said, smiling.

"Okay, so let's say since you hit twenty-one," Talon said, winking at her co-star.

"You are definitely trouble, aren't you?"

"Only the best kind," Talon said, a wicked sparkle in her eyes.

Riley laughed softly at the younger woman, shaking her head.

"Can we do this?" Legend asked, her voice edgy by that point.

Riley glanced at her and noted that the script she held was shaking slightly. There were also dark circles starting to show up under her eyes. Riley had heard that Legend hadn't slept the night before.

They read through the scene until Legend was satisfied with the nuances of it; it was the portrayal of Georgia and Lizette's first meeting on the track infield on base. By midday they were ready to start filming. Legend called action, and Riley and Talon went through the scene. Legend cut it and reset it three times, wanting different angles to work with for editing. When she cut for the final time, Riley could see that her hands were shaking badly.

"Can we take a break?" Riley asked.

Legend nodded, getting out of her chair and walking away from the set. By the time Riley caught up to her, Legend was halfway to her bungalow.

"You're not sleeping at all, are you?" Riley asked.

Legend didn't answer, just continued toward her bungalow. Riley followed her, undaunted. Legend threw open the door and walked over to her nightstand, where she opened the drawer.

"How much of that are you taking?" Riley asked as she closed the door behind her.

Legend halted her motion of opening the bottle, closing her eyes for a long moment.

"I don't need a mother, Riley," she said without turning around.

"You obviously need something," Riley said softly.

"Yeah, I need you to get out so I can do what I need to to get through this fucking day, okay?"

Riley pressed her lips together, surprised at the stab of pain in her heart. She leaned against the door and said nothing.

Thinking that Riley had left, Legend opened the bottle and popped the pill before replacing the container in the drawer. She stood with her hands on the nightstand, her head bowed, her eyes closed as she breathed slowly. She was doing her best to get a handle on her emotions, which were raging. She remembered the day like it was yesterday—she remembered Georgette's smile; she remembered the feeling of pure joy at having someone to talk to for a change. It tore at her, making her feel raw and so desperately lonely again.

As she turned around, she still had a look of utter devastation on her face. Riley saw it and sucked in her breath in shock. Without stopping to think about it, she strode over to Legend and took her in her arms, just wanting to take away the pain she saw on her face. As she put her arms around her, she half expected Legend to shove her away. She was, therefore, surprised when Legend put her head against Riley's shoulder and slid her arms around her waist, shaking from the raw emotions she was feeling. In that moment, Riley was Georgette, and Legend held on to her for dear life.

They stood that way for a number of minutes. Riley smoothed her hand over Legend's back, her other hand holding her head.

"This is hard for you," Riley whispered. It wasn't a question; it was a statement.

Legend blew her breath out audibly, swallowing convulsively.

"Please let me help you," Riley said softly, her lips right next to Legend's ear.

Legend didn't answer, turning her head and kissing Riley's neck softly.

"I'm okay," she said quietly.

Riley closed her eyes. She knew that wasn't true, that it was what all addicts thought. She hugged Legend tighter, afraid to push her anymore, thinking she'd shove her away then. Riley knew she was the only one that was close enough to Legend on set to try and help her. She resolved to talk to Finley about what to watch for and do everything to keep this incredibly talented woman from truly damaging herself while she made this movie.

After a long while, Legend stepped back, her look still haunted but less devastated. Turning around, she opened the door and gestured for Riley to precede her, not quite meeting her eyes. Riley walked out of the room, happy to note that Legend followed her. The rest of the day was spent walking through other scenes, including Lizette's first meeting with her commanding officer.

They wrapped filming by five that afternoon. It had been a long day.

The next day things got really rough. They filmed not only the first time Lizette and Georgia kissed, but also the first time they made love. Riley watched Legend become more and more withdrawn during the read through. Legend called a break and said they would film the love scene after lunch. Riley had thought she'd be nervous about the scene between her and Talon, since she'd actually be naked for part of it, but she spent the entire lunchtime worried about Legend, who'd disappeared.

When the break was over, Legend reappeared, looking winded and sweating. The filming of the scene went quite smoothly, and Legend called for no retakes. When she yelled cut, Riley heard her voice break. Before Riley could get her robe on and grab her clothes, Legend had once again disappeared. Throwing all caution to the wind, Riley asked everyone if they'd seen where she had gone. Someone finally said they'd seen her take off running, and pointed in the direction of the desert that lay beyond the set area. Riley grabbed someone and told them to get a car and head in that direction, and then checked the rest of the set in case Legend had already returned or the person had been wrong. She was frantic an hour later when she couldn't find Legend. She kept picturing finding her lying dead somewhere; she had to mentally force the image away over and over again.

By the time Legend showed back up, she was dripping sweat. She went straight to her bungalow and took a shower. She was just dropping onto her bed, wearing sweats and a tank top, when Riley walked in.

"Jesus! Where have you been!" Riley exclaimed, walking over to the bed. She could see that Legend was moving like she was in pain; she was shaking and her muscles kept contracting.

"Legend…" Riley said cautiously. "Talk to me. What's going on?"

Legend blew her breath out, shaking her head. "I can't… I… I need to even out…" she said, her tone pained.

Riley nodded. "Okay, how do we do that?"

"Need to get rid of this energy," Legend said. "Tried to run it off… Couldn't run anymore…" She swallowed convulsively, making a pained sound.

Riley leaned down over her, searching Legend's face. "What else can we do?"

Legend shook her head, breathing heavily now, her muscles still contracting.

"Should I get the medic?" Riley asked.

"No!" Legend exclaimed. "They can't know... I can't..." she said, trailing off as she let out a low moan. "It'll kill the film."

Riley reached out, touching Legend's face, turning her head to look into her eyes. "Tell me what I can do," she said, her face hovering just above Legend's.

She was shocked when Legend pressed her lips to hers in a desperate kiss. When they parted, Legend moaned again. Riley couldn't tell if it was pleasure or pain. Taking a chance, she leaned down to kiss Legend again, sucking gently at her lips, eliciting yet another moan from her.

"Take what you need, Legend," Riley said.

Legend's hands were at her waist instantly as her mouth captured Riley's again in a passionate kiss. Legend dragged Riley's body closer, moaning as their lips met over and over. Then she was pulling at Riley's clothes. Riley helped remove them, keeping the contact of their kiss as much as she could, feeling her body responding mightily to the heat of the situation. Before long she was naked, and Legend was pulling off her own clothes, her hands already moving over Riley's body possessively.

Legend's lips left Riley's to travel over her skin, grasping at her waist, pulling her closer, pressing against her. As they closed over a rock-hard nipple, Riley cried out, feeling her body coil tightly, ready to release at any moment. Legend's fingers sliding between her legs made her scream as she came, grasping at Legend's shoulders, saying her name over and over again, pressing closer as the orgasm went on and on and built again and again.

When Legend finally lay back, Riley lay half over her, feeling like her body was still on fire. Legend's body still moved sensually underneath her.

"I need to…" Riley said, her hand on Legend's stomach.

"You don't…" Legend said, shaking her head.

"You're still pulsing, Legend," Riley said, lowering her head to kiss Legend's skin, moving to a hard nipple, her hand sliding lower.

As her mouth closed over Legend's nipple, her hand barely touching the slick wetness between Legend's legs, Legend began bucking and gasping in her release. She grasped at Riley, pulling her closer, grinding her body against her.

"God… God…" Legend chanted in her release.

It excited Riley further to hear Legend's complete release and feel how wet she was. She moaned against her neck, and felt Legend move to put her on her back, sliding her body between Riley's legs and grinding her pelvis against Riley's pussy. Before long they were both coming again.

Legend moved slightly to Riley's side, breathing heavily, but her body was finally stilling.

Riley turned her head, looking at Legend's face. Her eyes were closed.

"Are you okay now?" Riley asked softly.

Legend opened her eyes; they looked more green than gold at that moment. Her mouth was set in an unhappy line.

"I'm sorry, Ri," she whispered huskily.

"For what?"

"For this," Legend said, gesturing to their bodies still intertwined. "For using you like this."

"I told you to."

"But you shouldn't have had to," Legend said sadly. "I bitch about people being professional, and I can't even manage to be."

"You are professional, Legend. You're going through hell right now, and no one is seeing it but me."

"But you," Legend said softly.

"You need an outlet for all of this," Riley said, gesturing to the set beyond the bungalow.

Legend looked back at her, sighing and shaking her head. "That doesn't make it right to use you as that outlet."

"Did I seem like I minded a few minutes ago?" Riley asked, her blue eyes sparkling in a challenge. "I remember coming right alongside you. In fact, I remember coming first… so…"

Legend gave a short laugh, smiling. "That's the difference?"

"Definitely," Riley said, happy to see the smile.

Legend nodded, nuzzling her lips against Riley's neck. Riley slid her hand up Legend's back, caressing her and feeling extremely sated. It seemed odd to her that she had no feeling of insecurity—no feeling like this was strange at all. She didn't know if it was because she'd grown so used to the way Kai and Finley were affectionate with each other or if she just cared about Legend enough not to feel strange. Regardless of the reason, she felt completely comfortable with Legend lying over her.

"When did you figure out you were gay?" Riley asked softly.

"About a year after I got into the Marines."

"This was during Don't Ask, Don't Tell, right?"

"Yep."

"That must have been really hard for you."

"It wasn't easy," Legend said. "It got a lot harder when I met Georgette."

"You were in the Marines for ten years, right?"

Legend nodded.

"When did you meet Georgette?"

"I was in year nine at that point."

"Oh," Riley said. "Did you have other relationships before her?"

"Nothing lasting. I avoided getting deeply involved—it was just too much work to hide it. So I had random sex, flings with women in passing, and never with anyone in camp, always outside of it, or someone passing through."

"But Georgette was different," Riley said. It wasn't a question.

"Yes, she was."

Riley nodded. She knew she shouldn't ask too many questions; she didn't want to upset Legend.

Legend lay against Riley, feeling warm and so completely sated and drained she found herself dozing off. She also found that she didn't want to move away, like she usually did after sexual encounters. She inhaled the scent that Riley wore, thinking it was very much her, soft and delicate.

Riley felt Legend's breath become even, and hoped she was falling asleep. She figured the crew had guessed by this time that they were wrapped for the day. Lying in Legend's room, she found herself dozing off as well. It had been an eventful day.

Chapter 4

"You ready for this?" Kai asked Remington.

They were in Kai's office, sitting at the computer.

Remington grinned. "As ready as I'm likely to get."

Kai hit the button to connect them to the girls in California at Kai's house via webcam. They both felt really weird, having never done this kind of thing before. When the girls picked up and they could see their faces, however, both Kai and Remington both smiled.

"There they are!" Wynter said, smiling. "Hi, babe!"

"Hey, honey," Remington said. "Is Memphis there?"

"I'm here!" Memphis said, leaning down to put her face to the camera with a grin.

"Hey, kiddo, how're you doing?" Remington asked.

"Fine. Our girls are freaking out though," Memphis said.

"Why's that?"

"She's listening to *The Heroin Diaries*," Wynter put in.

"Which is…"

"It's an album by a band called Sixx:A.M.," Memphis said. "It's pretty dark stuff, but I'm listening to it because it's the kind of vibe Legend is going for on the movie. I'm just trying to get into the mode, you know?"

Remington nodded. "They just love ya, kid. It's not their fault."

Memphis smiled. "I know."

"Hey, let's give Kai and Finley some air time here too," Remington said, shifting out of the way so Kai could get in the frame properly.

Wynter and Memphis moved, letting Finley shift into view.

"There's my handsome boi," Finley said, smiling brightly.

"Yeah, yeah," Kai said, rolling her eyes.

"Is that your office?" Finley asked.

Kai obliged her by moving to the side, then picked up the laptop to show her the rest. Finley didn't miss the fact that her picture lay on Kai's desk; it made her smile from ear to ear.

"What's that grin about?" Kai asked when she set the laptop back down.

Finley bit her lip, her eyes shining. "You have my picture there."

Kai smiled softly. "Of course I do," she whispered. "Remi has Wynter's picture too, but it's in her bunk at the room."

"Rat," Remington muttered.

"It gets a lot of attention," Kai said, grinning.

"Well, she's kind of famous, you know," Finley said.

Kai smiled. "Yeah, kind of."

"You have my picture?" Wynter asked from behind Finley.

"Of course," Remington said. "I opted for the one that wasn't poster-sized—figured too many men would be drooling and I'd have to kill someone."

Wynter laughed softly.

"Colonel," Kai's clerk said as he walked in, standing at attention and saluting.

Kai stood up, returning the salute. "Whaddya got?" she asked.

"Report, ma'am."

"Thank you," Kai said. "Dismissed."

Finley could see Kai reading the report as Wynter and Remington talked for a couple of minutes. Kai winced slightly, then took a deep breath, blowing it out.

"I gotta go," Kai said, setting the report on her desk and moving back to the camera. "I love you, babe. I'll talk to you later, okay?"

"Okay, Kai. I love you!"

After Kai had walked out, Finley saw Remington scan the report she'd left on her desk.

"Bondye…" Remington breathed.

"What?" Finley asked, instantly worried. "What happened?"

"There was a fatality. Two, actually," Remington said gravely. "She lost a man and a dog…"

"Oh my God!" Finley said, in tears. "This is exactly what I was afraid of."

"You need to be easy on this one, Finley."

"What do you mean, easy?"

"I mean that Kai takes every one of these hard, and the last thing she needs is to get blasted with your fears…"

Finley drew in a sharp breath, but then realized that Remington was right. If Kai already felt horrible about losing a man and one of their dogs, her pouring out her fears and worries would just pile that on to make Kai feel worse.

She nodded slowly. "I understand," she said. "You're right—I will just support her. Thank you, Remi."

"Byenvini," Remington said.

"That means 'you're welcome,'" Wynter said, shaking her head at her girlfriend. "Not everyone speaks Creole, babe."

"Sorry," Remington said. "Look, I'm gonna go make sure she's okay."

"Okay, babe, go," Wynter said. "I love you. Take good care."

"Mwen renmen ou," Remington said—*I love you.* "You too, Memphis. Don't give our girls too hard of a time, huh?"

"No, ma'am," Memphis said, smiling. "Love you!"

Remington clicked what she thought was the close button, but only minimized the screen. She left the office and located Kai standing outside, watching as they offloaded the bodies.

"What happened?" Remington asked.

"Wall collapsed," Kai said gravely.

"Damnit…"

Kai nodded. "First one this round."

"Hopefully the only one this round."

"Is Fin freaking out?"

"No, she's good. She understands." Remington didn't mention why Finley now understood.

"Gotta make the call," Kai said, turning to walk back inside.

Remington watched her go, shaking her head. Being in command wasn't always what it was cracked up to be.

Later that night, Finley called Kai. She answered sounding so far away and unhappy.

"How are you, babe?" Finley asked.

"We lost a soldier and a dog today."

"I know, I heard. I'm so sorry, Kai…"

Kai was silent for a moment, doing her best to push back the tears that wanted to come.

"This is the part that sucks," she said, her voice affected by the tears in her throat.

Finley's eyes filled with tears. "Yes, it does, but they were heroes, Kai. You're all heroes over there."

She heard Kai let her breath out slowly, and knew she was doing her best not to lose it completely.

"I miss you, babe," Kai said softly.

"I miss you too."

They were both silent for a few long moments.

"So you wanna hear the latest from Morocco?" Finley asked, hoping a change of topic would help.

"Is that where your mom is filming?" Kai asked, relieved for the chance to talk about something else.

"Yep. And apparently where she's sleeping with Legend Azaria now."

"What!" Kai exclaimed, startling a female reserve who was walking by. She mouthed *sorry* to the girl, who only smiled at her and winked flirtatiously. Kai just shook her head.

Finley was laughing. "Yeah, that was about my reaction too."

"How in the hell did that happen?"

"I guess Legend's really going through the wringer with this movie, and my mom is feeling very... ah... protective of her for some reason."

"Interesting..." Kai said, grinning. "Think she's gonna come back a lesbian?"

"I wouldn't put it past her," Finley said. "But I know that Legend's kind of known for seducing women, so hopefully my mom doesn't get her heart all wrapped up in her."

Kai grimaced. "Yeah, that might suck."

"Well, my mom knows how Legend is, and she's been around Hollywood long enough to understand film flings. Hell, she's had enough of them herself."

"Yeah, but..." Kai trailed off as she thought about the fact that it might be different, since it wasn't something Finley's mom had had experience with before.

"Sex is sex," Finley said. "I guess I'll just have to kind of keep tabs on Mom to make sure she's not getting her heart involved."

"Sounds like fun."

"Tell me about it. It's probably our fault, you know."

"How's it our fault?" Kai asked, dismayed.

"She's seen how happy you make me. Maybe she figures a butch like Legend Azaria can make her happy where no man ever has."

"That might be true if your mom was gay."

"Hey, maybe she's one of those late bloomers," Finley said, grinning.

"Oh Lord," Kai said, rolling her eyes.

"Well, you and Cassiana prove that it's in the genes…"

"Okay, so you're gay and you got it from your mom?"

"Maybe," Finley smiled. "So what's the weather like there?"

"Not too bad. Little cold tonight, down to about forty degrees."

"Oh, that's cold. I'd be freezing."

Kai chuckled. "I'd keep you warm," she said, her voice lowering an octave.

"Would you?" Finley asked softly.

"Mmhmm…" Kai murmured, feeling her body hum with desire. "Jesus… It's only been a week and I miss you so much."

"I miss you too. I'm having to do extra workouts to keep from killing someone at the hospital."

"You and me both," Kai said, chuckling. "Hey, when I get back, I want to take you up to Mendocino."

"I would love that."

"Then it's a plan. There's a great hotel with a view of the beach. When I have my travel orders to come home, I'll make a reservation."

"How long can we stay?"

Kai smiled. "As long as you want."

"I love you," Finley said softly.

"I love you," Kai said. "I better get off the line before my cell phone bill is as big as the house payment."

Finley laughed softly. "Okay. You stay safe, okay?"

"I will."

They hung up a few moments later. Kai looked around at the makeshift camp they'd built. It was in a clearing, but there were still buildings in the area that were damaged. She was trying to work with the Army Corps of Engineers to help shore up the ones closest to the camp. It didn't make her less nervous about them, but she hadn't made the call on where they set the camp; she'd come into that mess. Shaking her head, she walked back toward the barracks, pulling her coat tighter around her as the wind came up.

Georgette was excited about a solution she'd found for her and Legend's problem with spending time together without the possibility of discovery. She'd been driving around the perimeter of the camp and near the old part of the base. She'd noticed an old outbuilding that resembled a small house. Parking her Jeep, she'd gotten out and checked it out. It was an old supply shed, so it was secure enough, and it had a decent floor. Legend was on another week-long mission, so Georgette carefully set aside things to take out to the shed.

"I have something I need to show you," she said when Legend got back.

Georgette was sitting in a Jeep, so it was nothing for Legend to climb in. In ten minutes they were at the shed. Legend looked questioningly over at Georgette.

"Come on," Georgette said, smiling as she got out of the vehicle.

Legend climbed out and followed Georgette to the shed. Georgette threw the door open with a flourish. Legend stared openmouthed at the inside of the building. Georgette had managed to bring in a mattress, sheets, blankets, and a few other items including wine and glasses.

"What, no beer?" Legend asked, grinning.

Georgette poked her in the ribs with a fingernail. "No, we're going to pretend like we're adults."

"Adults drink beer, honey," Legend said, walking inside.

"Adults with class drink wine," Georgette said, batting her eyelashes.

"Oh, I see," Legend said. "And what led you to believe I have any class?"

"Two degrees from Stanford University," Georgette said, closing the door and sliding her arms up around Legend's shoulders.

"Just a school, babe—doesn't make me classy," Legend said, lowering her head to capture Georgette's lips hungrily with hers.

Georgette moaned immediately, pressing closer to Legend, loving the way that she made her feel. Within minutes they were making love, making use of the mattress on the floor. Afterward they lay together, both on their backs, Georgette's fingers laced with Legend's.

"What do you want to do when you get out?" Georgette asked.

"I don't plan on getting out."

Georgette glanced up at her, shocked. "You don't?"

"No, this is my career."

"But…" Georgette began, trailing off as she shook her head.

"But what?"

"How are you ever going to live a full life in the Marines?" Georgette let Legend's hand go so she could turn over to look down at

her.

"What's a full life?"

"You know, love, marriage, kids…"

Legend shrugged. "Kind of gave those up when I figured out I was gay."

"Gay marriage is legal in Massachusetts," Georgette pointed out.

"One whole state," Legend said, her expression cynical. "And that's a legislative action—the popular vote won't likely carry it."

"It's a start."

"George," Legend said, reaching out to touch her cheek. "It'll never be legal in the Marines, and that's the state I work for."

Georgette looked somewhat crestfallen.

"Besides, you said your family would completely freak out about this kind of thing. You think they'd go for you marrying a woman?" Legend reasoned.

Georgette shrugged. "I guess I wouldn't be asking them…"

"You'd break with your family for me?" Legend asked, dumbfounded.

"I love you," Georgette said simply.

"George, you gotta stop saying that," Legend said, shaking her head.

"Why?"

"Because you don't love me. You're just… lonely."

"So lonely I'd sleep with a woman?" Georgette asked sharply.

"George…"

"So lonely I'd break with every Christian belief I've ever held to be with you? Is that really what you think, Legend Azaria?" Georgette all but yelled as she sat up.

"Babe, calm down…"

"Don't tell me to calm down," Georgette said, her tone matching the narrowed look in her eyes.

"Okay," Legend said, sitting up as well and sliding her arms around Georgette. "Babe, I'm not trying to upset you."

"Well, then you're damned talented, because you're really pissing me off!" Georgette snapped as she started reaching for her clothes.

"George, wait," Legend said, putting her hand out to stop her. "Please, just wait."

"What?" Georgette said, turning to look at Legend—and that was when Legend saw the tears in her eyes.

"Oh, honey…" Legend breathed, reaching out to touch Georgette's cheek. "I'm sorry, okay? I'm sorry… I just…"

"You don't want me to love you, do you?"

Legend looked back at her, searching Georgette's beautiful blue eyes. Finally she blew her breath out, shaking her head.

"I see," Georgette said, nodding as she started pulling on her shirt. "I'm just someone to have sex with, nothing else. I see. Well, I don't think I can compromise my beliefs that much, Legend, not even for you."

Legend picked up her clothes and started pulling them on. Her heart was screaming at her to stop Georgette from leaving, but her head was telling her it was probably better if they stopped this now. Georgette left a few minutes later. Legend lay back on the mattress and *stared up at the ceiling, the ache in her heart threatening to overwhelm her.*

They'd filmed the scene in the shed that day, and Riley had seen the pain in Legend's eyes as she called for a cut. Fortunately, Legend had asked for a few retakes and then finally wrapped it for the day. Riley found her lying on her bed twenty minutes later. She kicked off her shoes and lay down next to Legend, putting her head against her shoulder. She glanced up and saw the grin that curled Legend's lips slightly, even as she put her arm around Riley's shoulders.

"You okay?" Riley asked after twenty minutes of silence.

Legend blew her breath out loudly. "It's amazing how you see how many mistakes you made when you review your life this way," she said softly.

"Everyone makes mistakes, Legend."

"Oh, but I make really good ones."

Riley sat up, looking down at Legend. "You think trying to keep her from loving you was wrong?"

"I think it cost us some time," Legend said, her expression haunted.

Riley nodded. "She didn't understand that you were trying to protect her."

Legend laughed humorlessly. "She thought I was using her."

Riley looked back at her, searching Legend's eyes. "Did she know about your previous relationships? Or lack thereof?"

"Yeah, she'd asked me at one point, before all of that between us started. I'd been stupid enough to tell her."

"Well, so she was just going with what she thought she knew about you."

"Right," Legend said. "And I let her think it. And I told myself it was to protect her."

"What do you mean, you told yourself it was to protect her?"

"I was protecting me too," Legend said disdainfully. "I was protecting my career in the Marines by letting her think that I didn't love her."

Riley knew she'd now found the source of pain. "Did you really know you loved her at that point?"

"I suspected it. I just really didn't want to see it."

Riley nodded. "Legend, that was new for you too. You can't expect to have handled everything perfectly."

Legend gazed at Riley. "Gonna excuse me one way or the other, aren't you?"

"I just think that beating yourself up about it now is only going to hurt you."

Legend sat up, her eyes now searching Riley's. "You sure you're not gay?" she asked, grinning.

"I'm not sure of anything these days," Riley answered honestly.

Legend's lips claimed hers then as she reached out, sliding her hand around Riley's waist to pull her closer. Riley felt her pulse quicken immediately. Legend's lips moved expertly over Riley's, sucking, then she slid her tongue between them sensually. Riley slipped her hands up to Legend's shoulders, grasping at them, as Legend further deepened the passionate kiss.

Riley gasped as she felt Legend's hands slide under her shirt, unclasping her bra and moving it out of her way, her thumbs brushing back and forth over hard nipples as she continued to kiss her. Riley moaned repeatedly against Legend's lips. After what seemed like hours to Riley, Legend pushed her back on the bed, taking the time to remove Riley's clothes but not her own.

Legend's lips moved from Riley's to her neck, sucking and biting at her skin, making Riley writhe, still grasping at Legend's shoulders. Legend moved lower, kissing and sliding her tongue over Riley's skin, her hands moving up over Riley's arms and shoulders sensually. When her mouth closed over a hardened nipple, Riley rose up, pressing her body against Legend's. Legend swirled her tongue around one nipple while sliding one hand over to the other, her fingers caressing and teasing it as she continued.

"Oh my God… Legend… please…" Riley moaned, never having been so excited in her life and wanting so much for Legend to touch her.

Legend moved lower, taking her time to kiss every inch of Riley's skin. Her hands slid over Riley's breasts, still touching and teasing nipples as her mouth moved sensually over her abdomen, then lower. Riley was gasping for breath at that point, her heart beating so wildly, her body straining against Legend's. She thought she'd explode when Legend moved down, sliding her hands over Riley's thighs, her mouth so close to Riley that she could feel her breath on her pubic hair.

When Legend's hands moved up her inner thighs, Riley tensed, wanting so much to feel Legend's mouth on her. Legend spread her legs wider and Riley thought she'd come right then and there. As Legend's tongue slid up her inner thigh, Riley reached out, touching Legend's head, wanting to pull her closer but also excited to see what she would do.

Legend's tongue touched the very top of her pussy and Riley was coming immediately. Legend held on to her leg, plunging her tongue into her then, and Riley was sure she'd just explode. She came so hard and for what seemed forever, and Legend continued to lick and touch her until Riley couldn't take any more. Then Legend moved back up her body, kissing her lips sensually.

"I can't even begin to think of a way to describe what you just did," Riley said, still out of breath.

"I went down on you," Legend said. "You can't tell me no man's done that before."

"Not like that! Jesus! Are you, like, considered some kind of cunnilingus master or something?"

Legend chuckled. "Like some kind of ninja or something?"

"Exactly!"

"I think I'd be considered above average," Legend said, grinning slyly.

"I'd say! Holy crap! This might be why my daughter walks around with a big smile on her face all the time."

Legend laughed. "I'd bet Kai's probably pretty good—with all that muscle, she'd have to be good at a few things…"

"Hmm…" Riley murmured, sliding her hand over Legend's arms. "You've got more muscle than I'd have thought."

"I'm stealth," Legend said, grinning.

"Why is it that I'm completely naked and you're dressed?" Riley asked, her eyebrow raised.

"Talent?" Legend said, her light eyes sparkling.

"Hmm…" Riley murmured again. "I think we're going to need to remedy that, but not before I get dressed and drag you over to get something to eat."

"There's going to be dragging?" Legend asked, raising an eyebrow.

"If you don't cooperate," Riley said, stretching sensually.

"You keep doing that and we're not goin' anywhere, babe," Legend said, eyeing Riley's body appreciatively.

"You're going to eat some dinner, Legend Azaria," Riley said, giving her a narrowed look, even as she reached for her clothes. "Do you have a middle name?" she asked as she dressed.

"Not one I'm gonna tell you."

"Why?" Riley asked, giving her a mockingly hurt look.

"'Cause I know you—you'll use it to nag me," Legend said as she got up off the bed.

"I don't nag you," Riley said, pulling her shoes on.

"What do you call it?" Legend asked as she took Riley's hand in hers to lead her out of the bungalow.

"Gentle prodding," Riley said, liking that Legend was holding her hand.

It didn't go unnoticed by the crew or cast either. Legend's eyes met every one of theirs mildly. Riley refused to look in any way ashamed. She knew why she was with Legend, and if people didn't understand or like it, that was their problem.

They were eating when Legend looked over at her. "Leora," she said simply.

"Leora?" Riley repeated. "That's your middle name?"

"Yep. It's Hebrew."

"What does it mean?"

"Light."

"Ustura Leora Azaria."

"Very good. Perfect accent."

Riley smiled. "I'm used to having to pick up accents quickly."

Legend nodded. "I've always liked that about your acting—you never phone it in on the accents. You nail them, every time. Even the American ones."

Riley smiled, warmed by Legend's praise. "Thank you," she said. "Most people don't notice."

"Well, I notice dedication to your craft. It's important to me."

"Because you're so dedicated to yours."

"I try to be."

"You succeed, Legend," Riley said confidently.

She reached out, putting her hand over Legend's, looking directly into her eyes. Legend grinned as she put her hand over Riley's. It was the first picture the world saw of Legend Azaria and Riley Taylor.

"Did you get the email I sent you?" Finley asked Kai the next time they spoke on the phone.

"No, what email?"

"Jesus, why does this call sound so tinny?" Finley asked. "Check your email—you have to see the picture!"

"What picture?" Kai asked, even as she pulled out her phone.

She found the email from Finley; the subject line was *OMFG!* Opening it, Kai saw the picture Finley was talking about.

"Holy shit…" Kai muttered.

"I know, right!" Finley exclaimed, wincing at the feedback from her phone. Getting up from the kitchen table, she walked outside, hoping to improve the connection. It worked.

"I dunno, Fin. She looks pretty damned happy there," Kai said.

"I know! That's what I'm worried about," Finley said, sitting down on one of the chaise longues.

"Legend looks pretty happy too," Kai observed.

"Yeah, but…"

"Your mom is pretty awesome, Fin. Maybe she's actually captured Legend's heart—you don't know for sure."

"Kai, I know Hollywood, okay? I grew up around it, and I know what happens with players like Legend Azaria. They stomp all over women like my mom."

"Hey, that's not fair. Your mom's probably broken more than a few hearts in her time too."

"I know, Kai," Finley said. "But those were men, and… they knew what they were getting into when they got involved with her."

"And you think she doesn't know what she's getting involved

with, with Legend? You said so yourself—she knows all about Legend's reputation. She's going into this with her eyes open. And I note that you're not too worried about Legend getting hurt," Kai said pointedly.

Finley winced. She hadn't even thought of it that way; all she was worried about was her mother.

"Fin," Kai said when she didn't answer. "You didn't think about that, did you?"

"No," Finley said, her voice suddenly very small.

"Because Legend's a butch, you assume she's going to do the heart-breaking."

Again Finley winced, because yes, that was exactly how she'd thought.

"Our hearts are just as breakable, babe," Kai said softly.

Finley took a deep breath, blowing it out slowly. "I'm sorry, Kai. I should know that by now, shouldn't I?

"Yeah," Kai said evenly.

Finley bit her lip. She'd been the one who'd broken Kai's heart when she'd hesitated to tell Kai that she loved her and had avoided talking about moving in with her. Kai had been the one who'd been hurt by that, not her. She'd never dated a butch lesbian before, because she was afraid a butch would want to control her, because she'd fallen for the stereotypes. Kai was nothing like any woman she'd ever met, let alone dated. And yet, here she was assigning those same stereotypes to another butch she hardly knew. She knew why Kai was irritated with her.

"I'm sorry, babe," Finley whispered, feeling her heart in her

118

throat.

"Your mom can take care of herself," Kai said. "She's been doing it for a long time."

"I know. I guess I just don't want to see her get hurt, and especially not by one of our own, you know?"

"I know, but we can't control that, honey."

Finley nodded. "You're right. I know, you're right."

"Okay, I gotta go. We're headed out on patrol and I need to get this report out before we go. I love you."

"I love you. And, Kai…"

"Yeah?"

"I really am sorry about what I said."

"It wasn't what you said, baby—it's what you thought. You're going to marry a butch, and you're going to have to get this bullshit stereotype out of your head at some point."

"I know. I will. I'll work on it. I'm going to marry a butch…" she said, sounding thrilled at the prospect.

"Yes, you are," Kai said, smiling softly.

"I love you so much, Kai."

"And I love you. I gotta go, babe."

"Okay, bye."

"Bye."

They hung up. Finley walked back inside, and was finishing the dishes when she heard music. It was the song Kai listened to all the time by Linkin Park, called "Castle of Glass." She looked around, trying to figure out where the music was coming from. As she got close to the laptop, she realized that was the source.

"How'd that happen?" Finley muttered.

She assumed that somehow iTunes was on and running a playlist. But iTunes wasn't open. She looked down at the toolbar and only saw one icon with a bar under it to indicate it was active. It was the Skype icon. She clicked on it and was stunned to be looking at Kai. It was obvious that Kai wasn't seeing her, because she was tapping away at the keyboard on her laptop, her head moving to the music on her iPhone next to her.

At first Finley thought she should say something to let Kai know that the webcam was still active, but then she realized she was getting to see Kai in real time... and being a Marine. The temptation to watch her was just too much. Finley reached over and muted the mic on her side so noise from her end wouldn't translate to Kai's computer. Then she sat down at the table and got to watch Kai at work as a colonel for the US Marines—and oh, what a glorious sight it was.

Kai scanned whatever she'd just typed, making faces at either the computer or whatever she'd just read.

"Damnit," Kai muttered. "Sands!"

"Ma'am?" replied a female voice from not too far away.

"What's another word for *invade*, that doesn't sound so... invasive," she said, grinning at her lack of creativity.

Apparently Sands found it amusing too, because she laughed. "Try *occupy*! It's working for those idiots sitting on Wall Street, right?"

"Oorah," Kai muttered as she began typing again.

"Did that work?" asked the woman's voice, closer now.

Kai grinned. "Yes, I think it makes our influx of young people sound a bit less dire."

"Don't want them issuing a strike order or anything."

Finley narrowed her eyes as she saw a female hand touch Kai's shoulder. She was happy to see Kai's eyes widen slightly, and when Kai sat up, she displaced the hand. She also saw Kai glance over to where Finley's picture was pinned to her board.

"I need to finish this up," Kai said, her tone more official suddenly. "Can you go check to see if the unit is assembled?"

"Yes, sure," Sands said.

Finley heard the door close. Kai blew her breath out. "Sometimes DADT came in rather handy…" she muttered.

Finley laughed—her girl was definitely one of a kind. She wasn't really surprised by this Sands being interested, but it was obvious that Kai was not interested in her. And Finley took heart in that. She found that she loved Kai even more for what she was seeing while Kai didn't know she was being observed. There was a bit of guilt that she was essentially spying on Kai, and she knew she'd need to tell her about the webcam, but for those few minutes, she found that it was wonderful to be able to almost touch Kai. It made her entire day. She was also extremely touched that when Kai got up to leave, she looked over at the picture again, kissing her finger; Kai touched the picture, her expression soft. Finley knew that had she not already been madly in love with Kai Marou Temple, she would be at that point.

Kai walked out to where her unit waited with their dogs.

"Mount up," she said, taking the dog she was working with from her second-in-command.

She nodded over at Remington, who stood with her unit, ready to follow the K9s. Remington nodded back.

They were assigned a set of buildings to search, and Kai and her unit worked through them with the dogs. Donning gloves, they pulled debris away to let the dogs get closer and check for bodies as well as possibly live people.

At one point, they saw a group of people moving toward the unit. One of them was exclaiming something in Italian; Kai glanced over at the one person in her unit that spoke the language.

"What's he saying?" Kai asked, even as she held up her hand to Remington and her unit, who'd already started to move toward the group with their weapons at the ready

The man listened to the Italian, nodding. "He said there's someone calling for help down the street."

"Okay," Kai said. "I'll go. Remi, come cover me."

"Ten-four," Remington said, turning to her unit. "Stay here, keep your eyes open."

Kai signaled her dog to follow the man. She reached back, touching her weapon in its holster. It was there if she needed it; she never fully trusted anyone while she was doing her job.

The man led them down the street, and Kai could definitely hear muffled cries. The dog, an Italian greyhound, signaled right away on a particular area of the building. Kai got on her radio.

"King Bravo, come in."

"Yeah, Colonel?" came the reply.

"Head down here. We have a live one—bring three members with you."

"Ten-four, Colonel!"

Kai immediately started pulling debris away, grabbing bricks and rebar. Before long the people in the group were helping. Shortly after that, four men in her unit were there as well. Remington was also helping, keeping her rifle no more than an arm's length away.

Before long they were pulling a young girl out of the debris.

"Get a medic down here!" Kai yelled, and heard the radio call shortly thereafter.

She knelt down and picked up the girl, since her feet were bare and there was glass everywhere.

The girl threw her arms around Kai's neck. "Grazie, grazie!" she exclaimed over and over again.

One of her unit took a picture with his phone. Another was taking video as the people in the group that had approached them hugged Kai and the rest of the unit, including Remington. They were jubilant, chanting, "USA, USA!" It was a very happy moment.

Kai told Finley about it the next day when she called her.

"Oh, I need to see that picture and the video, Colonel…" Finley said, smiling.

Kai grinned. "Ma'am, yes ma'am."

"That's really cool, babe—it really is. I'm glad you guys had a good day," Finley said, then paused. "Um… I have something I have to tell you."

"What's that?" Kai asked, leaning against the wall of the barracks.

"Yesterday, I discovered something."

"And what's that?"

"Well, I think when Remi meant to close the Skype connection on your laptop the other day, she only minimized the screen…"

"So what does that mean?"

"It means I could see you yesterday in your office," Finley said, biting her lip.

"Oh," Kai said simply.

"Yeah… I thought I should tell you—I didn't want to, like, spy on you or anything," she said. "But can I ask you a really huge favor?"

"Okay, what?" Kai asked, still puzzling through the webcam thing.

"Can you leave it on?" Finley asked hopefully.

"Why?" Kai asked, mystified.

"Because… I felt like I could almost touch you. It was nice to just be able to see you doing stuff, even the cute faces you make at the computer…"

"Uh-huh," Kai said, sounding like she was rolling her eyes—which she was.

"It was just nice to see you, babe. You didn't feel as far away suddenly."

Kai sighed. "How can I say no to that now?"

"I'm really hoping you can't…" Finley said, letting her voice trail off.

"I'm not always in the office, you know."

"I know, I know, but just to see you when you are would be wonderful," Finley said. "Cassie'd probably get a kick out of it too."

"Okay, you win. I'll leave it on," Kai said, smiling. She was unable to fathom why Finley would want to watch her do boring office work.

"Yay! Thank you, honey!" Finley said, smiling from ear to ear.

Kai chuckled. "Try not to make me regret it."

Chapter 5

Legend managed to avoid seeing Georgette for three weeks, taking every possible mission or way around the office to avoid her. The day she finally had to go into the office, she turned in her report for her last mission and handed over her footage to her commanding officer. She was just leaving, glancing around to make sure Georgette wasn't around, when she walked right into her; Legend's hands shot out to steady the other woman before she fell.

"I'm sorry," Legend said, very aware that they were in the middle of the office.

"It's okay," Georgette said, averting her eyes.

Legend let Georgette go, stepping back and then walking around her. She headed straight out the doors and broke into a dead run; half an hour later she found herself at the supply shed. She leaned her head against the wall for a full five minutes, catching her breath. Then she walked inside. She took off her BDU jacket and then her shirt, because it was soaking wet with sweat, stripping down to only her exercise bra. She took off her boots and socks in an effort to cool her body down. It was the hottest part of the day in the desert and not the time to be running like a mad woman. She lay down on the mattress, staring up at the ceiling blindly.

Legend was startled awake when someone touched her arm. She realized she must have fallen asleep. She looked up to see Georgette kneeling next to her.

"George? What? How?" she stammered.

"I saw you run," Georgette said. "When you left the office, I saw you take off running. I took a chance that you'd come here."

Legend sat up, her eyes guarded.

"I know what you're doing," Georgette said.

"What do you mean, what I'm doing?"

"I mean, you're trying to protect me," Georgette said. "From messing up my career."

"What makes you think I'm not trying to protect mine?"

Georgette looked hesitant for a moment, but then nodded. "I'm sure you're doing that too."

Legend didn't answer, putting her knees up to her chest, her arms around them. It was an unconsciously defensive gesture.

"You want me to believe that I'm just another one of those girls you sleep with," Georgette said.

Legend's lips twitched, but she didn't say anything.

"I know that's what you want me to think." Georgette sat back on her heels, putting herself at eye level with Legend. "But I don't believe it."

"Why not?" Legend asked blandly.

Without a word, Georgette took Legend's face into her hands, leaning in and kissing her so tenderly that Legend felt her heart lurch. She started to pull back, but Georgette held her fast, kissing her again

"George, stop," Legend said sharply.

"No," Georgette said simply, leaning in for another kiss.

With every touch, Legend could feel another section of her armor ripping away.

"Please…" she pleaded, shaking her head. "Don't…"

"I love you," Georgette said, kissing her again. "I love you, Legend," and another kiss. "I love you…"

Legend gave something between a moan and a cry, and wrapped her arms around Georgette, capturing her lips in a deep, soulful kiss that left them both breathless. Pulling back, Legend looked into Georgette's eyes.

"I love you," she said, feeling completely bare and beyond vulnerable. She was shaking with the sheer terror of it.

"I know you do," Georgette said.

They made love for hours that afternoon, not returning to camp until the middle of the night. Fortunately they'd both been off duty, so no one had truly missed them.

Legend fell asleep in her bunk both terrified and thrilled beyond belief.

Riley made her way to Legend's bungalow after washing off her makeup and putting on regular clothes. They'd filmed yet another rough scene that day, and she knew Legend would be hurting. Things between them had been going smoothly. Riley noted that Legend seemed to be sleeping better and using less. She seemed less agitated. For herself, Riley was astounded at how good it felt to be around Legend. They were able to talk on so many levels. Legend hadn't been in the movie business for her entire life, but she'd had enough experience with it to understand a lot about what went on. Legend was very personable, and laughed easily when she wasn't stressed. She was also an excellent lover, and Riley was completely shocked by her own body's reaction to everything Legend did to her.

She'd never imagined herself as a lesbian, but she could easily see how she could get drawn into someone like Legend Azaria. With her dynamic personality and wild streak, she was just exciting enough to make Riley feel exhilarated to be around her. By the same token, when she wasn't using, Legend could sit calmly and quietly, simply holding Riley, with them both lost in their own thoughts. Their relationship was both comfortable and exciting.

Riley walked into Legend's bungalow, looking toward the bed; predictably, Legend was lying on it with her arms up over her face. Riley crossed the room and lay down next to her, putting her hand on her stomach.

Legend grinned, dropping one arm to encircle her shoulders.

"Rough one, huh?" Riley said.

"Yeah..." Legend said, breathing out slowly. "Sometimes I actually forget how good she was at getting around my defenses."

Riley nodded. "It seems like she was pretty determined to be with you."

"Despite everything I told her, she just never believed it."

"About not loving her?"

"No, about what the Marines would do if they caught us," Legend said, her voice thick with emotion.

Riley wanted to ask what exactly had happened, but she knew Legend would have told her already if she'd wanted her to know. There was a definite sense of dread from everyone on the cast and crew. It was obvious something had happened; the fact that Georgette was nowhere in evidence in Legend's life spoke to a few possibilities. It was also well known that Legend had been discharged from the Marines for "conduct unbecoming an officer." One of the tattoos she had on her left arm was a stylized set of letters, *CUO*, with a knife slashing through them and blood dripping from the hilt of the blade into a pool of rainbow blood. Riley had asked about the letters, and Legend had told her what they meant. It had only confirmed what people believed.

They lay together for a while, until Riley heard her phone ping. She pulled it out.

"What's up?" Legend asked when Riley made a slight noise at what she'd read.

"A bunch of the cast and crew are headed into Rabat to go to some club," Riley said, putting her phone away.

"You're going with them, aren't you?"

"Are you really up to going out?" Riley asked doubtfully.

Legend blew her breath out, shaking her head. "No, but that doesn't mean you can't go, babe."

"I don't want to leave you here alone."

Legend made a sound in the back of her throat. "I'll be fine. Go."

"Legend…" Riley began, shaking her head.

"Jesus, I'm not a complete head case," Legend said, a little bit of annoyance coloring her voice. "I can handle a night alone." She softened her expression. "These are your cast mates. It's probably good for you to hang out with them too. You spend all your time with me— that doesn't help the chemistry between all of you."

Riley bit her lip. She didn't want to annoy Legend by refusing to go because she was worried about her. By the same token, she knew that Legend did better when she was around. Part of her worried that she was trying to get her to go so she could indulge.

"What are you going to do while I'm gone?" Riley asked, trying to keep the suspicion out of her voice.

It was obvious she hadn't quite succeeded when Legend's eyes narrowed slightly, but then she shrugged.

"Probably get drunk and pass out," she said honestly.

"Well, that sounds fun."

"I didn't say I was going to have fun—I said I was going to get drunk and pass out," Legend said, her tone amused.

Riley nodded. "Okay, fine. I'll go, if you're sure."

"I'm sure."

Riley went with the group to a place called La Cabane Bambou, Al Yacoute, a nightclub that played a mix of disco music and eighties stuff. There was a dance floor and multiple rooms with different color themes. Naturally, the minute they all got there the paparazzi weren't far behind, having heard that the cast and crew from the latest Legend Azaria production were out for the night.

Talon leaned over to Riley at one point. "Maybe we should give them something to talk about…"

Riley gave her a sidelong look, a smile on her lips. "Like what?"

"Like this," Talon said, leaning over far enough to kiss Riley on the lips. Cameras clicked away.

"Are you insane?" Riley said, grinning up at her.

"Hey, we're supposed to be a couple in the movie. Believe me, this will sell it."

Riley looked thoughtful, thinking that the film deserved every second of attention it could get, since Legend was pouring her life's blood into it.

"Just so long as you remember who I'm with," she said, her expression serious.

"How could I forget?" Talon said, her green eyes sparkling.

They spent the evening dancing, laughing, and drinking. The paparazzi covered every second of it, and before they even headed back to the encampment, pictures were all over the internet.

Legend was halfway into a bottle of scotch when she looked at her phone. Pictures of Riley and Talon were all over Facebook and every gossip site possible. Her lips twitched, her eyes narrowing when she came to one that depicted Talon and Riley dancing—Talon had her hand on Riley's ass. Setting her phone aside, Legend picked up the bottle and drained it, then threw it across the room. She lay staring up at the ceiling, feeling the alcohol move through her veins. She opened the nightstand and took out a bottle of pills, popped one and then dropped the bottle back into the drawer. The top fell off and the pills scattered. Legend didn't care; she just closed the drawer and lay back, waiting for the pill to take effect.

When Riley got back to the camp, she checked on Legend. She just poked her head into the room, not wanting to wake her if she was sleeping. She saw that Legend was indeed asleep on her stomach, her arms around the pillow under her head. Riley decided to leave her be for the night, and went back to her room to wash off her makeup and take a quick shower. As she lay in her own bed for the first time in a couple of weeks, Riley found that she missed Legend's warmth next to her, and her arms around her. She fell into a fitful sleep.

Finley heard Imagine Dragons' "I Bet My Life" coming from the laptop, which told her Kai was in the office. She went over to the computer and opened the Skype window. She couldn't help but smile at the screen. There was Kai sitting at her desk. At first Finley couldn't figure out what she was doing, but then she heard Kai muttering.

"Okay, can they make the eye of this friggin' thing any smaller?"

Finley noticed that Kai wasn't wearing her uniform, but a white dress shirt and her brown leather jacket.

"That doesn't look like Marine issue," Finley said, and saw Kai jump slightly. "Sorry, babe!" she added, chuckling as Kai opened the Skype screen.

"Damnit, I forget that thing's on all the time," Kai said, grinning. "And no, this isn't Marine issue. The people in the village here have invited all of us down to a meal, and of course the one decent shirt I have with me is missing a button."

"And that's you over there trying to sew?" Finley asked, grinning.

"You know," Kai said, narrowing her eyes, "don't make me turn this off…"

"No, no!" Finley said, laughing. "I'll stop making fun of you right now."

"Uh-huh."

"So you brought regular clothes with you too?"

"You always bring civvies, babe," Kai said. "You don't always want to look like a Marine when you're deployed."

"Why the hell not? You look so damned sexy in that uniform, I can barely stand it…" Finley said, trailing off as she shivered.

Kai raised an eyebrow. "And you want me running around the area looking like that all the time?"

"Well, you look damned good right now, too. Now I'm thinking I should have put a ring on your finger before you left."

"You had your chance…"

"That's cold," Finley said, laughing.

Kai laughed too; Finley loved the sound of it.

"So they're making you all dinner?" Finley asked.

"Yeah. It'll be nice to eat some real food—the mess here is awful. The MREs are almost better."

"That's bad, huh?"

"Oh yeah."

"Colonel," Sands said, walking into Kai's office.

"Yeah," Kai said, glancing up at the woman.

"There's two—Oh, I'm sorry," Sands said, seeing Finley's face on the computer screen.

Kai grinned. "It's okay, Sands. This is my girlfriend, Finley. Finley, this is Sands."

Finley narrowed her eyes slightly, even though she smiled. "Nice to meet you."

"Um, you too," Sands said, looking taken aback, her eyes straying back to Kai. "There's two guys here—they said there's a problem with procurement."

"Okay, send them in," Kai said, then looked at the screen again. "Babe, I'm gonna minimize for a minute, okay?"

"Okay," Finley said.

Kai stood up as two men entered. They both snapped to attention and saluted Kai, who returned it.

"At ease. What's up, guys?"

"We're getting a backup here for a couple of our requisitions, Colonel," said one of the men, the shorter of the two.

"Okay. Any idea why?"

"Dunno, but it's happening up the food chain," the other man said.

"What are we low on?"

"Food for the dogs," the first man said.

Kai raised her head, her eyes narrowed slightly. "Have you checked with command?"

"No, we wanted your AOK to do that," the first man said.

"You have it. How low are we?"

"Low. Maybe a couple of days' worth."

"Son of a…" Kai muttered. "Okay, you get on the horn today. If you don't get a resolution, you come see me. I'll get my own damned credit card out if I need to."

"Yes, ma'am," the second man said, his expression both surprised and impressed. "Thank you, ma'am," he said, saluting her again.

After the men had left, Kai sat down again, an odd look on her face.

"What's that look about?" Finley asked.

Kai chuckled, opening the screen again so she could see her. "Just kind of a feeling," she said.

"What kind of a feeling?"

"A sense of déjà vu…" Kai said, trailing off as her expression turned contemplative.

"With?"

Kai glanced at the screen again, shaking her head slightly. "Sorry, babe—just with requisitions for the dogs getting held up. It's happened before, when someone was trying to get my attention."

"Someone being…" Finley said, having a feeling she already knew.

The way Kai looked at her said it all.

"Seriously?" Finley said. "You think it's Kathy? But how? I thought she got out."

"She did, but she could have joined the reserves too… I dunno."

"It's probably just a coincidence," Finley said hopefully.

"From your lips, babe."

"Go eat real food, babe, and don't worry about this."

"Okay," Kai said, grinning. "Love you."

Finley smiled. "Love you!"

"Are you hungover?" Cat asked Jovina when they talked the day after the night in Rabat.

"I am a little bit," Jovina said, smiling as she lay back on her bed. Their report call wasn't for another hour. "How are things there?"

"Same old, same old," Cat said. "I miss you though."

Jovina closed her eyes. "I miss you too, minha linda," she said— *my beautiful* in Portuguese.

"Oh… she's pulling out the Portigi," Cat murmured. "So was there anyone interesting at that club last night?"

"You mean other than Riley and Talon?"

Cat laughed. "Yeah, we already saw the pictures back here. I thought Riley was dating Legend."

"She is. I think that stuff last night was for the cameras."

"Seriously?"

"Yeah," Jovina said. "It generates excitement for the movie, people thinking that they're actually a thing… you know?"

"And you think people aren't going to wonder what happened with Legend?"

"People think whatever the tabloids tell them to think."

"Not the intelligent people."

Jovina laughed. "That's true."

"Think Legend's gonna think that?"

Jovina hesitated, having not thought about that, but then shrugged. "I'm sure she knows how this stuff works. Besides, I don't think it's like true love or anything. It's one of those film flings."

"Film flings?" Cat said, sitting back in her office chair.

"Yeah, a romance that lasts the duration of making the film. It's pretty common."

Cat narrowed her eyes. "I don't think I like you working in an industry that promotes that kind of thing…"

Jovina laughed again. "I don't do it, babe. I have my girl."

"Yes, you do," Cat said. "Talon come on to you again since that first time?"

"No," Jovina said seriously. "She knows I'm in love with this really sexy cop type back home."

Cat grinned. "Cop type, huh?"

"Uh-huh. And she also knows that it wouldn't be a good idea to piss you off."

Cat nodded, narrowing her eyes slightly. "Good." She looked up as Raine walked up to her door. "Babe, I gotta go," she said. "I love you."

Jovina smiled. "I love you."

Riley wasn't sure what had happened, but Legend had suddenly gone completely cold on her. The next morning, when they began shooting, Legend was short with her, and wasn't smiling at all. At the lunch break Riley tried to talk to her, but she was busy talking to Jovina and Tula the entire time. When they began shooting again, nothing she did was what Legend wanted. Legend finally called a wrap for the day and walked away from the set. Riley went to wash off her makeup and change clothes and then headed for Legend's bungalow. She knocked this time, afraid to just walk in for the first time in weeks. There was no answer, but Riley was sure Legend was in there, so she opened the door quietly.

Legend was lying on her bed, curled almost into a ball; it was alarming. Riley strode over. Both of Legend's arms were up in front of her face, as if shielding her from something.

"Legend…" she said softly.

"Get out."

"What is wrong?" Riley said, kneeling next to the bed.

"I said, get out."

"Not until you tell me why you're acting this way," Riley said, searching what little she could see of Legend's face.

"Last time I'm gonna tell ya…"

"You can tell me as many times as you want, Legend. I'm not leaving until you talk to me," Riley said, her voice stronger.

She could see the muscles in Legend's jaw jumping as she clenched her teeth, and then there was the telltale twitch of her muscles contracting. Tears appeared in Riley's eyes instantly.

"How much did you take?" she asked, looking toward the nightstand drawer.

"Apparently not enough," Legend growled.

"Legend…" Riley began, reaching out to touch her arm.

Legend knocked her hand away. "Don't fucking touch me."

"What the hell is going on!" Riley snapped, shocked.

"Just get out," Legend said, her tone dull and lifeless again.

"I'm not leaving."

"I can make you leave."

"Try," Riley said, moving to sit down on the bed, her arms crossed in front of her chest.

Legend didn't respond, simply continued to lie as she was. At one point her body contracted again, and Riley had to force herself not to say anything. She opened the nightstand drawer and saw that the pills from the red bottle were all over the inside. She knew the red bottle contained whatever Legend took to come down from the speed. She began putting the pills back into the bottle, doing anything to keep herself busy. She was trying to ignore the urge to shake Legend for getting back into this spiral, and desperately wanted to know how much of the garbage the woman had taken.

She took out her phone and texted Finley, asking what would happen if Legend had taken too many of the pills to bring her down. Finley responded that she would likely be tired, irritable, that her speech could be slurred and her pupils would be dilated. She also told Riley to watch her breathing, saying the drugs could repress her respiratory system. Lastly, Finley said that it was possible that Legend could become suicidal. It was the very last thing Riley wanted to read.

She spent the better part of the night watching Legend carefully, making sure she was breathing, covering her up with a blanket when she started to shiver uncontrollably. She tried again and again to get Legend to talk to her; Legend wouldn't answer her, but she didn't threaten to remove her from the room anymore either. Riley ended up sitting on the bed, behind where Legend lay, her upper body curled over the top of Legend's, trying to keep her warm when she started to shiver again. She rubbed Legend's arms soothingly, doing anything she could think of to get her through the drugs in her system.

Early the next morning, Riley lay on the bed next to Legend, with her hand on her back so she could feel for her breathing. She hadn't slept all night, too worried about Legend to do so. She was just dozing off when Legend moved to turn over, her eyes a mixture of gold and green in the small slit of sunshine coming through the curtains.

"Why are you still here?" Legend asked evenly.

"Because you worry me."

Legend stared back at her for a long moment. "Aren't you worried Talon will miss you?"

Riley gave Legend a stunned and confused look. "What are you talking about?"

"I saw the pictures."

Riley opened her mouth to ask what pictures, but then realized exactly what she was talking about.

"Oh my God, Legend!" Riley said, exasperated. "That's what this is all about?"

Legend just looked back at her.

"We did that for the cameras. To help promote the movie."

"Her hand on your ass was promoting the movie?"

"Oh Jesus, it was probably there for a fraction of a second and they caught it on film. Jesus fucking Christ, Legend, you know this business!"

Legend stared back at her.

Riley reached up, touching her face. "There's nothing between me and Talon. Christ, you should know that." She shook her head. "You see us every day on the set. She's a sweet kid, but she's a fucking kid!"

"You two looked pretty cozy."

Riley sighed. "For the cameras—only for the cameras. She knows I'm with you."

"Are you?" Legend asked softly.

"Yes!" Riley exclaimed. "Yes," she repeated more softly, touching Legend's face, looking into her eyes.

Legend looked like she was trying to assimilate what she was hearing. Riley leaned in, kissing her softly, holding it until she felt Legend begin to respond. When Legend reached up to pull her closer, Riley sighed. They were making love a minute later, and Riley found that Legend was much more aggressive this time—and she also found that that excited her no end.

"I didn't like seeing you with her," Legend said quietly as they lay together afterward.

"It wasn't real."

"I didn't like it."

"I'm sorry."

"As long as you're on this set, you belong to me," Legend said possessively.

Riley shuddered at the sound of her voice, as well as in response to the words. She nodded, kissing Legend again.

They lay together for a while, then Legend moved, shifting to Riley's side—that was when Riley saw the dark mark on her neck.

"Oops," Riley said, grinning as she touched it.

Legend's lips curled into a grin. "You might wanna look in a mirror before you get too proud of yourself," she said, her tone as mischievous as the look in her eyes.

Riley levered herself up, looking in the mirror across from Legend's bed. There was a dark mark on her neck, much darker than Legend's. She turned and glowered down at her.

"I don't know if the makeup artist can even cover that," she said.

"Then don't give me a reason to mark you as mine again," Legend said simply, her stare possessive.

Riley's eyes widened. She'd never had anyone talk to her that way, and she found that it excited the hell out of her. She realized that she really wanted to be possessed by this woman—it was a completely new feeling for her. Moving to cover Legend's body with her own, she leaned down and kissed her hungrily. Legend responded instantly, reaching up and grasping a handful of Riley's long hair and pulling her closer, her lips moving hungrily over Riley's in an almost bruising kiss. Riley grasped at her, wanting everything she was doing and more.

They made love again, and by the time they lay trying to catch their breath, they both had marks on them. Neither of them complained one bit—it had been a fiery session of make-up sex.

Things on set were much better that day. Although everyone noticed the marks, no one was stupid enough to say anything. The makeup artist did her best to hide the blemishes on Riley's fair skin; Riley couldn't stop grinning the entire time.

They were lying in the shed, having just made love for the second time that morning.

"Oh, I almost forgot," Georgette said, levering herself up on her elbows to look down at Legend.

"What?" Legend asked, smiling.

"I got into radio communications!"

"You did?" Legend asked, her eyes sparkling.

Georgette nodded. "I told my CO that was what I wanted to do, and he finally approved it! I'm so jazzed!"

Legend laughed. "You should be, babe. That's fantastic."

"It's all because of you. You gave me the courage to do it."

"I just said you should try. You did it."

"But you being so good at your job, and making them rethink how valuable we women are, is what gave me the courage."

Legend smiled softly.

They'd been together for seven months by that time, and things were going great. There was always the looming question about what would happen in their future, but they avoided talking about that. Legend had just been promoted to major, and she was thrilled. Finally she was receiving some credit for her work. It only served to cement for her that the Marines was her career. Georgette finally getting an opportunity to do what she'd wanted to do was yet another step in the direction away from their relationship. Legend refused to look at it too closely. She was enjoying being in a relationship with this gorgeous, easygoing woman, and she didn't want to fuck it up by talking too seriously about the future—a future that was uncertain at best, disastrous at worst.

"When do you start tech school?" Legend asked.

"Next week," Georgette said, stretching her arms above her head. "I'm so excited I can barely stand it!"

Legend watched her stretch, feeling her body respond to the sexy sight.

"Well, I've got another long one coming up," she said. "They've got me headed out to do some aerial work."

"Lucky!" Georgette said, shaking her head. "Guess I should have gone to college so I could get a cool job like yours, huh?"

"Hey, you're getting your cool job."

"Yeah, but it's not like yours. I still won't get to go outside the wire."

"Going outside the wire isn't all it's cracked up to be, babe. You get shot at, and it's dirty and hot, and you deal with men all day and night long."

"You just don't like the dealing with men part."

"You got that right," Legend said. "Speaking of which…"

"What?"

"You might want to… um…" Legend said, stammering as she tried to figure out how to say what she needed to. "Well, think about going out on some dates while I'm gone."

"Dates?" Georgette asked, stunned by the suggestion.

"Babe, you need to keep up the premise that you're straight. I have my bullshit story about a guy back home—you don't. So if you don't start doing at least a little bit of dating, they're going to start wondering why."

"That's not fair. The men aren't scrutinized for not going on dates!"

"Well, they are scrutinized if they don't talk about pussy-hunting on a daily basis," Legend said. "That's how a friend of mine got his ass kicked out."

Georgette stared back at Legend. "So you're telling me I should go out with some guy?"

"I'm not telling you to sleep with anyone. I'm just saying that you should go out with a couple of different guys and just say it didn't work out. At least then you have those on your scorecard, you know?"

Georgette looked mutinous. Legend leaned in, kissing her.

"I know, it sucks," she said. "But if we want to keep our careers, this is the kind of shit we need to do."

Georgette nodded, clearly unhappy about the prospect.

They'd filmed the scene in the shed that day, and Riley could easily see that Legend was getting agitated. She didn't understand it; the conversation had seemed so benign during the scene. She understood after lunch when the new pages were handed out. She immediately went looking for Legend.

It took her twenty minutes, but she finally found her leaning against one of the buildings. Her shirt was soaking with sweat, which meant she'd been running. She was smoking, her hand shaking as she lifted the cigarette to her mouth.

"Legend…" Riley said, walking up to her and into her arms.

Legend hugged Riley to her, closing her eyes and trying to draw strength from the other woman. She desperately wanted to run away at that moment, just get away from everything, but she knew she couldn't.

When Riley stepped back, she could see how haunted Legend

looked.

"Tell me what you're thinking," she said.

Legend gave a short, humorless laugh. "I'm thinking I'd like to get the fuck out of this desert right now…"

"Okay," Riley said. "But we just got the pages for the next major scene…"

Legend nodded, looking down at the ground, blowing out a stream of smoke.

The scene that they'd received was mostly set direction, showing Georgia and a man named Kitchings. They'd gone on a date, he'd bought her drinks, she was resistant to his charms, and he decided to help her loosen up. He'd dosed her with Rohypnol, a street version he'd gotten in town. She was a lot easier to handle after that. He'd taken her out back and taken her roughly. She'd awoken lying on the floor of the bathroom of the officers' club. She knew she'd been raped, but had no idea how to handle it. The last part of the scene was Georgia standing in the shower, trying to scrub every inch of her skin to get him off her, to the point of bruising and blood. It was horrendous.

"What are you thinking about in terms of the scene?" Riley asked, aware that it was the reason Legend had been so agitated during the filming of the previous scene.

"You mean, like it's my fucking fault?" Legend asked roughly, her lips quivering as she held back tears. "Yeah, it's my fault."

"It's not your fault. You couldn't know that pig would do that to her."

"I could have kept her out of the situation in the first place. I'm the one that told her to go out on dates."

"And you think she didn't have a choice about that?"

Legend blew her breath out, shaking her head.

"Legend, you couldn't control everything," Riley said beseechingly.

"I fucking knew what could happen."

"How could you know?"

Legend just looked back at her, her eyes flickering as she lifted the cigarette to her mouth again.

"Are you saying…" Riley said, trailing off because she couldn't even think of Legend being violated like that without wanting to throw up.

"It was years before, and the guy didn't succeed. And I seriously wonder if he could ever have kids after that, but… I knew what could happen."

"Still," Riley said, relief flooding her veins. "Maybe this is a scene you should leave to the assistant director."

Legend shook her head as she lit another cigarette with shaking hands.

"I need to do it. I need it to… It has to look right—it has to feel right."

"Legend… it's going to rip you apart."

Legend gave a quiet snort, her expression already devastated. "Yeah, probably."

"Then let the AD do it. You can look at the dailies to make sure she captures what you wanted."

"And that's going to be easier?"

"You won't have to suffer through retakes…"

Legend took another long drag of her cigarette, her hand shaking badly.

"Your hands are shaking a lot," Riley said.

"It's withdrawals. It's my body screaming for more."

"What can we do about that?"

"Give it more," Legend said simply.

Riley pressed her lips together. "Please let the AD do the scene, Legend. Please."

Legend stared back at her, seeing the plea in her blue eyes. Eyes so much like Georgette's. It hit her then that she'd not only be watching "Georgia's" rape; she'd be watching the woman she was currently seeing in that role. She felt like she was actually going to be sick. Bending over at the waist, she blew her breath out slowly.

She shook her head. "I don't know if I can fuckin' do this…" she said, trailing off as she shook her head again. "Why didn't I know how hard this was going to be? Living all this again…"

Riley stood by, devastated for Legend and what she was going through. She wasn't sure why Legend was so determined to tell this story, but she tended to think it would be better for her in the long run to work through the whole thing. At least, that's what she hoped.

"Please use the AD," Riley said again. "Otherwise, why did you bring her?"

Legend gave a short, sarcastic laugh. "In case I managed to OD during filming."

"That's not even sort of funny, Legend," Riley said, alarmed.

Legend shook her head. "I'm sorry." She knew it was a lousy thing to say to the woman who was trying desperately to keep her from doing just that.

Riley put her arms around Legend again, resting her head against her shoulder. "Please let the AD do the scene."

She felt Legend inhale deeply, then nod slowly. "I'll go talk to her now."

"Thank you," Riley said, hugging Legend tighter.

In the end, it was an awful scene to film, and Riley found herself getting very emotional. She had to do retake after retake, because she kept getting overwhelmed. The assistant director was extremely patient, giving her all the time she needed to get it right, knowing that she was close to Legend and that her loyalty stemmed from there.

When the scene was done, Riley washed off her makeup, changed her clothes, grabbed a bottle of Legend's favorite scotch, and went to her bungalow. They got drunk together and made love half of the night.

Chapter 6

Finley had started recording the webcam sessions, so she could watch them when Kai wasn't in the office. She knew she was probably crazy, but she felt like she wasn't missing as much time with Kai by seeing her whenever she wanted.

She was forever getting a laugh out of some of the conversations that went on between Kai and some of the men in her unit. There was an entire discussion about why marshmallows were better toasted than not toasted. Kai was forever chuckling over one of the guys who would yell from the other side of her office door, which was open half the time. Finley could see that she was a damned good leader.

One of her men was having issues with his girlfriend back home. Kai listened to his whole story and then explained the way she saw things. He asked her questions, and she answered them according to the way she thought. In the end he thanked her profusely for taking up her time with his "nonsense"; Kai simply grinned. "You come see me whenever you need to," she'd told him.

On one occasion, Finley found herself the topic of conversation, and she got to see Kai in full Marine colonel mode. She had been sitting at her computer, typing away, when a man came in. She'd returned his salute and asked what he needed, when his eyes strayed over to the picture of Finley.

"Holy shit, who's the hottie?" he asked, leering.

Kai's expression had immediately turned ice-cold. "That is my fiancée."

"You get to tap that? Good fucking job, Colonel! That's a prime piece of ass there," the man said as he winked at her.

Kai's eyes narrowed as she looked down at his left hand. "You married?" she asked.

"Yep," he said. "My sweet little Ellen's back home in Michigan."

"And would you want me to refer to your sweet little Ellen as a hot piece of ass?"

"Well... no..." the man said, looking shocked.

"Then what makes you think it's okay to refer to the woman I'm in love with in anything but the most respectful terms?"

"I... Well..." the man stammered, suddenly realizing his error and that he was now in deep shit.

"If you ever talk about a woman like that again in my presence, I'll have you on report so fast it'll make your head spin. You got that, Private?"

"Y-yes, ma'am," the man said, paling significantly.

"Now, tell me whatever it is you need to and get the hell out of my office," Kai growled.

Finley was so completely proud of Kai and the fact that she not only respected her but did so enough to insist that others do the same. She knew that sometimes "locker room talk" was just that, but the fact that Kai didn't feel the need to do it to fit in or be accepted by anyone was amazing. It made her love Kai even more, if that was even possible.

They were filming a series of field ops with Talon and the guys playing her unit. It had Legend and the crew out in the desert a lot. After four or five days, it was becoming obvious everyone was tired. Legend called it a wrap. She'd been awake for days again, doing rewrites and obsessing about the final scenes of the movie. She had her headphones permanently plugged into her ears and sat for all hours of the night writing in her notebook and making edits to screen directions, even for some of the shots that had already been done. She also spent hours reviewing the dailies, making notes, making changes, ordering reshoots.

Riley was at her wits' end. She knew Legend was using heavily again, and she couldn't seem to get her to back off it. Whenever she tried to get Legend to sleep or eat, she would get irritated and Riley would back off, afraid to really make her mad. She worried constantly about her, and whenever she talked to Finley, she barely talked about anything else.

Finley was getting worried about her mother, afraid that she was getting far too involved in Legend's turmoil, and afraid that if Legend went down, she'd take her mother down with her. She'd seen enough addiction in her time as a doctor and a resident to know what it could do to not only the person using but the people around them. The last thing she wanted was for her mother to get damaged by Legend's use.

One night on the way home from the gym, Finley got a phone call from Kai.

"Hi!" she answered happily.

"Hey, honey," Kai said, sounding tired.

"Oh, babe, when's the last time you slept?"

"I try, babe. It's just hard with so many people in a room."

"You guys are in with the rest of the crew now?"

"Yeah, we needed the other space for more supplies."

"Did the supply issue get resolved?" Finley asked hopefully.

"No. I used my credit card and bought extra in case it takes too long to get sorted. I can't not feed the dogs."

"I know, babe, I'm not questioning that," Finley assured her. "Still don't know what's going on?"

"No, but I've put in a call to HQ myself, raising holy hell. This shit is getting ridiculous."

"No kidding," Finley said, shaking her head.

"So what's going on with your mom?" Kai asked, having heard about the pictures of Riley with Talon Valois.

"Supposedly that was just acting for the cameras."

"Well, she's going all out for the team, huh?" Kai said, not sounding pleased.

"She's really committed to the movie and Legend Azaria…" Finley trailed off, and Kai could detect the displeasure in her voice.

"Why do you say it like that?" she asked.

Finley sighed. She hadn't really wanted to burden Kai with her worries. She debated saying anything, thinking it was better just to let Kai do what she needed to and not have to worry about Riley too.

"Fin?" Kai said when she didn't answer.

Finley sighed. "It's nothing. I'm just a little worried."

"Worried about what?"

"I don't want to bug you with it."

"Tell me."

"I'm just worried about my mom, that's all."

"Okay. Why?"

"Because she says that Legend is using heavily again, and I'm worried that when Legend finally snaps she's going to take my mom out with her."

Kai grimaced at the phrase Finley had used. "Does your mom think it's possible that she's going to snap?" she asked.

"I don't think my mom has any idea how volatile a junky can be."

"We're calling Legend a junky now?" Kai asked, surprised.

"If she's using as much as my mom said, Kai, she's a junky."

Kai pressed her lips together in consternation. "Okay…"

"Mom says that something's building, and they're just not sure how this movie ends, and Legend's getting more and more on edge about it. She's basically manic at this point."

"Is that standard for the drug she's using?"

"For speed? Yeah, it is, and if she's using a lot, it means her body is needing more and more. If she doesn't come down from it, she's going to kill herself, basically."

"Maybe that's what she's trying to do," Kai said unhappily.

"That's what I'm worried about."

"And you're worried your mother will get her heart broken."

"Yes," Finley said. "Or worse."

"Worse?"

"Addicts can… Let's just say they can take a lot of people out in their implosion."

"And you think that's where Legend is headed?"

"I don't know… I'm just really worried."

"I understand, babe, but there's not a lot you can do from there, so try to give your mom all the information she needs, and then trust her to be smart."

"I know. You're right," Finley said, blowing her breath out slowly.

"I'm sorry I'm not there," Kai said softly.

"I wish you were here too, Kai, but you're on the phone with me and that's helping too. I love you. Thank you for dealing with me and my psychotic paranoia…"

"You love your mom," Kai said. "It's okay to be a bit psychotic and paranoid, just so long as you understand there's only so much you can do."

"I'll work on that part," Finley said, nodding. "So how are things there?"

"Okay," Kai said, her tone telling Finley instantly that there was something she wasn't saying.

"Kai…" Finley said. "You made me tell you…"

"Okay, okay. We're having some aftershocks again."

Finley winced. It wasn't what she wanted to hear, but she knew she couldn't make Kai feel bad for telling her.

"Please, just be careful, babe," she said.

"I will, honey, promise," Kai said, happy that Finley wasn't going to unload all her worry onto her at that point.

It was one thing to know that the woman you loved was worried about you, but hearing all of their fears and concerns put those fears and concerns onto the person they were worried about. It was an extra burden to carry around all the time, and something Kai didn't need when she had so many people to worry about under her. Not the least of whom was Remington, who she knew she needed to bring home safe for Wynter and Memphis.

Legend got back from a two-week mission. She and Georgette met out at the shed. When they made love, Georgette jumped a little in response to Legend's touch.

"What's wrong?" Legend asked, immediately concerned.

"Nothing, just a little bit a chafing—you know, PT in the desert sun and all," Georgette said, leaning in to kiss her again.

Later, as they lay together, Georgette told her all about her tech school training and how interesting it was. Legend told her about the aerial mission and the footage she'd gotten.

"I'd love to see it," Georgette said, smiling. She knew Legend was always happy when she got good footage of battles and areas of conflict.

Legend noticed the shadow in her eyes, and wondered about it.

"So, did you do any flirting while I was gone?" Legend asked gently, aware that it wasn't something Georgette had wanted to do.

"I went out on two dates."

"Were they awful?" Legend asked, grimacing.

Georgette shrugged. "They were… dates," she said, her tone indicating she wasn't interested in talking about them.

Legend dropped the subject, figuring it was enough that Georgette had gone out with men; it would take some of the suspicion off them.

Three days later, Legend overheard Kitchings talking about nailing this hot blonde. She edged closer, listening in on the conversation. Kitchings went on to tell his buddies how the blonde was in his class at tech school and how hot she'd been for him.

"She totally came on to me. I knew she was into it."

"So was she good?" one of the other men asked.

"She was alright," Kitchings said, sounding bored.

"You still seeing her?" another guy asked.

"Oh yeah, I'm sure I'll be tapping that one again soon."

"Which one is she?" the first guy asked.

"You know, that hottie from the secretarial pool."

Legend's blood ran cold. It was everything she could do to get out of there without punching Kitchings in the face. She wanted to go and confront Georgette immediately, but she knew she couldn't. She started walking toward her barracks, her stride long. Yanking off her BDU shirt, going down to a tank top, she threw it aside and started running.

The anger pumping through her veins sent her further and faster. She paid absolutely no attention to what was around her; she just kept running, even when her legs screamed at her to stop. She kept running when she was in the middle of the desert with nothing around her but sand. All she could picture was Georgette with Kitchings, fucking him…

"I should have known… I should have known. No wonder she was sore. What the fuck is wrong with me!" she screamed to no one, yelling so loud her voice became hoarse.

She never saw the sniper; she just felt the impact of the bullet that threw her to the ground. She lay in the sand, bleeding, staring up at the sky and thinking maybe this was it, how it all ended. Part of her was okay with that. She could feel herself losing consciousness, and it occurred to her that she probably shouldn't let herself drift off, but part of her thought it didn't matter.

"Who cares? No one. No one," she muttered. She was unconscious a moment later.

She woke in the hospital back at the base. Apparently she'd been spotted running out into enemy territory, and although it had taken time to get someone after her, they'd finally come and had seen her lying bleeding in the sand.

Georgette had heard that a Marine had been shot. When she'd finally discovered that it was Major Azaria, she just about lost her mind. She'd gone straight to the hospital and had made a huge fuss to see the major. She'd finally been allowed to see Legend, who had been unconscious at the time. She'd sat, crying hysterically, by her bedside. It had been very obvious that she was distraught; the fact that she was holding Legend's hand created the only suspicion they needed to start an investigation.

Legend Azaria had shown up and intimidated enough men on the base to create some serious enemies. Some had just been waiting for the chance to nail her to the wall. Georgette gave them the perfect opportunity.

It was two days before Legend regained full consciousness, and by

159

that time the investigation was in full swing. She was informed of it the minute she opened her eyes. She lay in the hospital bed wondering why she hadn't just died in the desert like she should have. At least then she would have died a hero. Now they were just going to nail her to a fucking cross and kill her slowly.

Georgette walked in, her expression grave.

"What were you thinking, running into the desert like that?" she asked, her look searching.

"I was thinking that I wanted to kill either you or Kitchings, or both," Legend said simply.

Georgette paled. "What?" she asked tonelessly.

"I overheard him bragging about nailing you."

Georgette's lips trembled as she sat down heavily in the chair next to Legend's bed. "He said that?" she asked tremulously.

Legend glanced over at her, searching Georgette's eyes. "Yeah, that's what he said. George... what aren't you telling me?"

Georgette pressed her lips together, tears in her eyes.

"I didn't sleep with him," she said. "He drugged me and raped me."

Once again, Legend's blood ran as cold as ice. She started to get up from the bed.

"Legend, you can't!" Georgette exclaimed, putting her hands out to stop her.

"I'll fucking kill the son of a bitch," Legend growled, reaching up to rip out the IV.

"Stop!" Georgette yelled.

Every head in the place turned toward them.

"Please stop…" Georgette said, tears in her eyes.

Legend stilled, feeling sick suddenly and just wanting the pain to stop for a minute.

"Jesus, George… I'm so sorry…" she whispered hoarsely.

"They're going to eviscerate us, aren't they?" Georgette said, tears spilling over on her cheeks.

"Well, probably me. You might be able to skin by."

"I don't want to lie about us," Georgette said, shaking her head.

"George, you do what you have to in order to save your career," Legend said, her voice a harsh whisper. "I don't care what you have to say. Hell, say I forced you if you have to."

"No," Georgette said. "I won't do that."

"There's no reason for us to both go down. There's not going to be any saving my career—it's over for me. But you can still save yours. Do what you have to."

Georgette shook her head, tears streaming down her cheeks.

Legend felt dizzy suddenly. Closing her eyes slowly, she felt wetness at her back. She'd ripped open her stitches in an effort to get up and was losing blood again. She was unconscious a minute later; the last thing she saw was Georgette's face hovering over her.

It was two weeks before Legend got out of the hospital. By that time they were ready to take away her commission. The first thing she did was track down Kitchings.

"What do you want, dyke?" he said when she approached him, grinning at his buddies.

Legend punched him in the mouth so hard she felt his jaw crack. She walked away, feeling a little better in that moment.

"You broke his jaw?" Riley asked.

Legend nodded, her eyes reflecting the hatred she'd had for the man that had raped Georgette.

"I wish I'd killed him."

Riley's eyes widened. They'd just been given the scene before lunch. Riley had tracked Legend down again, finding her sitting at one of the tables in the chow hall, smoking and drinking coffee, her foot moving in agitation. She was, as usual, scribbling in her notebook. Things were building, and Riley was getting more and more concerned about Legend's state of mind. She had no idea where the story was going to end up, but she knew without a doubt that it did not have a happy ending.

She and Legend still spent some nights together, but they rarely talked. They had sex, and fell asleep next to each other, but Legend was always up and gone a couple of hours later. One morning after Riley woke up, she looked into the drawer with the pills. She was shocked and terrified to note that a lot of them were gone. Legend was having to consume more and more in order to keep getting the effect, and it was at dangerous levels. Riley just hoped that the movie would wrap before she managed to put herself in the hospital, or worse.

Stage Direction:

Lizette looks frantically for Georgette, checks barracks, chow hall, everywhere.

Lizette drives up to the shed. A second Jeep is there.

Lizette enters the shed. Georgia is lying on the mattress, asleep.

Lizette moves to wake Georgia. A medicine bottle drops from Georgia's hand.

Lizette: Georgia! <shaking Georgia> What did you do! <shaking Georgia again>

Georgia: <moans softly>

Stage Direction:

Lizette picks Georgia up and runs out to the Jeep, puts Georgia in, and drives back to the base.

Lizette runs Georgia into the hospital, screaming for help.

Doctors take Georgia and immediately start working on her.

After a few hours, Lizette is told they have saved her.

Lizette goes back to shed, finds suicide note from Georgia.

Letter is read in Georgia's voice.

Georgia: I'm sorry that I'm not strong enough to withstand what is to come for us. Please know that I love you and I'm so sorry that I cost you your career. You have been the love of my life. I regret nothing, except that I won't ever see your face again. All my love, Georgia.

Stage Direction:

Camera pans across the base. Lizette's

voice.

    <u>Lizette</u>: I never saw her again. She was sent home to her family, where I assume she lives today. As for me, I lost my commission, I lost my career. I was never brave enough to contact her; we'd both lost too much. Don't Ask, Don't Tell wasn't a safeguard for gays. It was a career killer, and it ruined lives. It's been estimated that at least 13,425 men and women were discharged under DADT. All those lives ruined, careers ruined, because of something that was no one's business. On September 20, 2011, Barack Obama repealed Don't Ask, Don't Tell, allowing gay men and lesbians to serve openly in the military for the first time ever. It was too late for Georgia and me, but it changed lives. This movie is dedicated to all those men and women who served their country under the cloud of DADT and did their jobs anyway. Thank you for your service.

It was the last scene of the movie. Legend called cut, and promptly left the set. Riley had to get changed and wash off her makeup. Everyone was expected to watch the dailies, which would include the final scene, an hour later. Riley hadn't located Legend in that time, but made her way to the building where the dailies were being run. She noted that Legend wasn't present, but as the dailies ended and the final scene was shown, everyone cheered. Riley looked around, hoping she'd just missed Legend walking into the building. She asked people if they'd seen her.

"I think I saw her near the chow hall right after we wrapped," Talon said.

Riley nodded, worried. Talon followed her as she made her way in that direction. Still she couldn't find Legend. She'd checked her bungalow before heading to view the dailies, thinking she hadn't been there because she was at the other building ahead of everyone else. She decided to go back to the bungalow, and Talon followed her.

As she approached the door, she could hear music playing. The song was Sixx:A.M.'s "Courtesy Call." Riley had heard it far too often around Legend. It was a very dark song that detailed a man overdosing on heroin and being found in a hotel by a maid. It always made Riley feel a little sick when she heard it. The chorus was the worst.

"This is just a courtesy call, this is just a matter of policy

This just an act of kindness, to let you know that your time is up."

A cold chill ran up Riley's spine as she opened the door. She knew she'd never forget the scene before her. Legend lay on the bed at an odd angle, indicating that she'd passed out. The red bottle was next to her, empty, and there was an empty bottle of scotch in her hand.

"Legend!" Riley screamed. "Talon!" she yelled as she rushed to the bed.

Talon moved past her, putting her hand out to touch the side of Legend's neck for a pulse.

"Riley, get the medic now!" Talon said. She picked Legend up and strode out of the room toward the medical station.

Riley ran ahead and hurried inside, screaming that they had an emergency. By the time Talon hit the doors, the staff were ready. Everyone was shocked to see that it was the film's director they were to work on.

The rest became a blur to Riley as tears flowed from her eyes. All she could think was that they'd saved Georgette—could they now save Legend?

Legend was flown to a hospital in Rabat in critical condition; they'd lost her pulse three times before the helicopter even arrived. Riley had climbed into the helicopter feeling a complete sense of unreality.

It was two days before Legend finally woke. She opened her eyes slowly, staring up at the ceiling for a long moment, then closed them again as she gave a low moan of despair.

Riley, who was sitting in the chair next to the bed, heard the sound and moved to Legend's side.

"Legend?" she said, touching her arm.

Legend's eyes opened again, and she slowly turned her head toward Riley.

"Why?" Legend asked, her voice barely a whisper.

"Why what?"

"Why… did… you… save… me?" Legend asked, her voice halting as she struggled with the effort to speak.

Riley was unable to fathom a response to that question. Her blue eyes filled with tears at the devastated look in Legend's eyes. She truly had meant to kill herself; her question had just answered that.

Legend shook her head slowly, blinking as unconsciousness sought to reclaim her. "Just… let… me go," she said softly, and was asleep again a moment later.

Riley stared at her, unable to believe what was happening. She talked to Finley a little while later.

"So she did it on purpose," Finley said, grimacing.

"Apparently," Riley said. "Not that there was much of a question about it, but I was hoping it was just a spur of the moment thing and she'd regret it when she woke up."

"Doesn't sound like she does."

"I don't understand," Riley said, shaking her head as she looked over at Legend lying in the bed.

"Mom, it sounds like she's had a pretty rough time of it. And for an addict, it's hard to see your way clear when the drugs are clouding your head," Finley said, wanting to offer as much support as she could.

"I just wish there was more I could do."

"This might be a job for professionals."

"She won't do that," Riley said, shaking her head. "She didn't want anyone to know about the drug use or the fact that this story is completely true to life."

"Seems like her secrets are starting to catch up to her."

Riley drew in a deep breath, expelling it audibly. "I don't want to lose her…" she said, her voice so soft and sad that Finley closed her eyes at hearing it; it was exactly what she'd been afraid of.

"You need to face the fact that you may not have any control over that, Mom," she said gently. She knew what she was saying was going to be hard for her mother to hear.

Finley was surprised to hear her mother sniffle, and realized she was crying. "Do you want me to come there?" she asked.

"No," Riley said. "You have Cassiana and everything to look after there with Kai away. I'll be okay. Thank you, though."

"If you change your mind, let me know. I can get Wynter or Quinn and Xandy to keep an eye on things here for me if needs be."

"Okay, honey," Riley said, smiling through the tears in her eyes.

She hung up then and resumed her vigil next to Legend's bed. She'd sworn everyone who had witnessed Legend's condition to secrecy; she just hoped it would work. She took Legend's hand. She couldn't believe that someone so dynamic and full of life could just as easily be so full of sadness that she would try to take her own life.

She supposed that was what had happened with Georgette, too—that things had just gotten to be too much and she'd given in to the desire to stop it all. Riley found that she was relieved to learn that Georgette hadn't succeeded in her attempt. It was just a lot to process.

"She what?" Kai asked Finley, sure she hadn't heard right.

"Legend tried to kill herself."

"Jesus…" Kai breathed. "I guess we were right on that one, huh?" she said, not sounding pleased with the prospect.

"My mom is so devastated, Kai. I think she's in love with Legend… or at least thinks she is. I don't even know where to begin on that."

"You said yourself that being gay can be genetic."

"I know, but… my mom has always drifted from one relationship to the next. And she usually bails when things get rough."

"And she's not bailing on Legend."

"No. Not yet, anyway."

Kai was silent, thinking how hard that must be. "I can't even imagine what she's going through," she said.

"I can't either," Finley said. "I offered to come there, but she told me it was okay."

"Are you going to do it anyway?"

Finley pressed her lips together, not sure how to answer.

"Fin?" Kai queried.

"I don't know, Kai," Finley said honestly. "I feel like I'd be invading Legend's privacy, you know? Mom says she was adamant about people not knowing about the drug use…"

"It's going to be obvious now."

"Mom thinks she's got everyone to keep it quiet. She's even planning to pay the hospital staff to keep Legend's condition a secret."

"Wow…"

"I know."

"Well, babe, it might be that Fate put Riley in Legend's path for a reason. Maybe she's meant to be the one that saves her."

Finley smiled. "Always an optimist, aren't you?"

"Gotta be when shit like this happens. Or you'll go crazy with wondering why someone talented like Legend has so much misery heaped on her."

"If that had happened to you—you know, getting caught and kicked out of the Marines for being gay—how would that have been for you?"

"It would have been devastating," Kai said. "The Marines was my life for a long time—I was dedicated to what I was doing. And I've seen what happens when they go after someone. They pick apart their life and the job they did. It's not pretty."

Finley nodded. "I'm so glad DADT got repealed."

"You and me both, babe."

"I wish it had happened in time for Legend and her girl."

"Maybe it wasn't meant to."

Finley sighed. Kai was able to turn anything to look at it in a positive light. "All I know is that I don't want my mom devastated by this," she said.

"Well, we'll just have to be there for her as much as we can."

"Yeah."

They talked about other things then, and hung up a little while later.

It was another day before Legend stirred again. She was highly agitated when she woke, and attempted to get out of the bed to leave.

"Legend, please!" Riley exclaimed, desperately trying to keep her from getting up.

"I need to go," Legend said, almost hysterical. "Let me go!"

"No!" Riley yelled, just as the nurses came in with a sedative.

"You can't," Legend said, seeing the needle. "You can't save me..." she said, even as the nurse put the needle into her arm.

She subsided then, and Riley sat back down. She knew this was just the beginning of withdrawals and that it would get worse before it got better. She was already looking into places that Legend could go to handle her addiction, but Riley was almost sure she wouldn't do it. It scared her.

Riley talked to the assistant director, who had taken the movie back to Los Angeles, where post-production was starting. Memphis was working on sounds and scores, and had had to pull in another person to help her, since Legend was unavailable. The assistant director was working on the editing, aware that Legend had set the shoot up to mirror the order of the scenes.

Things were proceeding on *For the Telling* regardless of Legend's incapacity. Riley was determined that she would stay with her, not willing to take the chance of her slipping away or forcing her way out of the hospital, only to succeed at what she'd failed to do the first time.

Two weeks later, after a number of bad sessions with Legend screaming to be let the hell out of the hospital and the doctors doing everything they could to help ease her symptoms, Legend was finally somewhat recovering. One afternoon she lay on her side, her arms crossed in front of her, her face partially covered. Riley glanced over and saw that Legend's eyes were open.

Setting aside the paper she was reading, Riley leaned forward, brushing Legend's hair back off her face. "How do you feel?" she asked softly.

Legend didn't answer at first, rubbing her face on her arms in mild agitation. "Like I got run over by a truck," she said eventually, her voice gravelly. "Like, ten times..."

Riley pressed her lips together, sympathy in her eyes. "It'll get better."

Legend didn't say anything, regarding Riley for a long minute.

"Why are you still here?" she asked.

Riley's expression became pained. "Because I want to make sure you're okay."

Legend gave a soft, humorless laugh. "I'm not okay."

"Can you tell me why?" Riley asked softly.

Again Legend rubbed her face on her arms, her eyes shadowed and unhappy. "Because this isn't where I expected to end up."

"Where did you expect to end up?"

"With George," Legend said simply.

Riley was perplexed. "But... how would you end up with her by doing what you did?" She didn't want to use the words "tried to kill yourself," because it would have made it too real.

"Because that's what she did..."

"But you said she survived."

"The script said she survived," Legend said, her voice taking on a haunted quality, as did the look in her eyes. "I lost her that day..." She trailed off as tears glazed her eyes.

Riley also had tears in her eyes instantly.

"Oh my God... Legend..." she said, her heart breaking all over again for this woman and all she'd suffered through.

She reached out, touching her arm, trying to soothe her. Legend was now crying soundlessly, tears slipping from her eyes. Fortunately, sleep reclaimed her then, but Riley couldn't escape the sad realization that Legend had lost Georgette to suicide, and she had tried to do the same thing to join her. It made her heart ache for them, for everything they'd lost.

Over the next couple of days, Legend was extremely quiet, but she was also calmer. The one thing she said was that she wanted to go home. Riley talked to the doctors, and they said they felt comfortable releasing Legend from the hospital. They also said that she needed drug treatment, but Riley didn't bother explaining that Legend Azaria wasn't likely to do that. She simply made arrangements for a private plane to take them both home to Los Angeles.

Kai was sitting in her office, working on a report for command, when Sands called to her.

"Colonel!"

"Yeah?" Kai called back.

"You have a general here to see you," Sands said, something odd in her tone.

"Okay," Kai said, getting to her feet, ready to come to attention and salute.

She wasn't completely shocked when Kathy walked in wearing civilian clothes. Kai stared back at her, her dark eyes narrow. She sat down at her desk and fiddled with a couple of things on the top of it, then looked back over at Kathy.

"No salute?" Kathy asked.

"You're not in uniform. I'm not required to salute you," Kai said, her expression completely calm.

"You don't seem surprised to see me."

"I had an inkling that something was going on at HQ that had something to do with you," Kai said. "You've been holding up my requisitions. Why?"

"Because I needed to get your attention, as usual."

"So you'll endanger my dogs and my people so you can get my attention?"

"I'll do what it takes to get what I want."

"So what do you want?"

"You know what I want."

"And what's that?" Kai asked, raising a dark eyebrow.

"I want you back in my bed where you belong," Kathy said, her blue eyes sparkling.

"And if I'm not interested?"

"You are, you just keep resisting it."

"I'm really not, actually," Kai said apathetically.

"You always say that, but your body tells me a different story," Kathy said, giving her a seductive look.

"Not anymore."

"Kai, don't lie to me. It's not who you are."

"I don't think you know who I am anymore, Kath," Kai said, a grin at her lips.

"Oh, I think I do…" Kathy reached out and put her hand on Kai's shoulder, sliding it downward.

Kai simply stared back at her, completely unaffected. She got back to her feet, her grin wry. Kathy moved to press herself against Kai, sliding her hands up her back sensually, a move that always proved effective. Kai simply grinned, her dark eyes sparkling with subdued humor.

"What the fuck?" Kathy exclaimed.

Kai turned her head, looking at the picture of Finley pinned to her board. "She's taken your place," she said contemptuously.

"Who the fuck is that?"

"That," Kai said, pointing her finger at Finley's picture, "is my fiancée."

"Your what?"

"You heard me."

Kathy stared openmouthed at the beautiful blonde in the picture. She was movie-star beautiful; Kathy knew she couldn't compete with that. Suddenly her confidence began to erode. She'd always had Kai; she'd always known that all she had to do was get close and she could get her back. Suddenly she wasn't so sure about that.

Kai sat back down, her legs set wide apart, her eyes narrowed.

"Now, get your ass back to HQ and approve all of my requisitions, or this entire conversation will be forwarded to command for their review."

"What are you talking about?" Kathy said, clearly confused.

Kai grinned. "This entire conversation is being recorded. You see, I have my webcam set up, and it's been recording us since you walked in here."

"You—"

"Careful, Kath," Kai said, her grin downright malicious now. "Unlike before, I can file on you for sexual harassment and creating a hostile work environment, and the Marine Corp will kick you out faster than you can blink."

Kathy's mouth fell open. She couldn't believe what she was hearing. Not only had she lost Kai to another woman, but now she was threatening to have her kicked out of the Corp?

"You wouldn't," she said, her last vestige of bravado on full display.

"Wanna bet your career, even in the reserves, on that?" Kai asked, her dark eyes widening slightly.

Kathy closed her mouth, pivoted on her heel, and walked out of the office, slamming the door.

Kai laughed, shaking her head. "Thanks, babe," she said, glancing at Finley's picture.

She told Finley about it when she called her that night.

"Oh my God. So she was the one holding your stuff up, just like you thought," Finley said, shaking her head.

"Yep," Kai said. "I did some checking, and she pulled a number of strings to get herself assigned as our oversight with the reserves at HQ. I hope it was worth it to her."

"What a bitch!"

"That she is," Kai said. "But I gotta tell ya, having that webcam up and ready to go was fantastic. All I had to do was hit the record button."

"Would you have really turned it over to your command?"

"Hell yeah. She's been pulling that shit on me since way back. It's about time it came back on her."

"Well, I'm glad you had it then," Finley said, smiling.

"So, have you heard from your mom?"

"Yeah, they're on their way home."

"Is Legend doing better?"

"Mom says she's been really quiet, but calmer."

"Is that an indication of better?" Kai asked, sensing from Finley's tone that it wasn't necessarily the case.

"It could be," Finley said. "Or it could be an indication that Legend Azaria knows how to lull people into a false sense of security."

"So you think she might still be suicidal, just pretending not to be so she can try it again?"

Finley grimaced. "Well, the thing about people who are serious about killing themselves is they don't talk about it—they just do it, like Legend did."

"So they don't threaten it to get attention—they just do it."

"Well, threatening doesn't always indicate that they want attention. It usually means they want someone to stop them, or help them, or at least try. It's a cry for help."

"But Legend didn't do that."

"Right, so it means she was pretty serious about doing it. I don't think that level of intent just goes away."

"But maybe it was the drugs that put her in that state of mind…"

"I don't know," Finley said. "Mom says she was getting more and more agitated as the movie got closer to wrapping up. She thinks it's because the woman Legend was seeing tried to kill herself—wait, correction, actually killed herself."

"Wait, what?" Kai said, not having heard the latest.

"Yeah, I guess she actually succeeded in killing herself. Legend just didn't write it that way for the movie."

"Damn…" Kai grimaced. "That's really rough," she said, trying to imagine how she'd feel in that situation. She was unable to even begin to think of how she'd handle it.

"I know," Finley said.

"No, babe… I don't think you can even imagine," Kai said solemnly. "For someone like Legend… like me… losing someone that we love and feel responsible for, like Legend must have felt for her girl—that's so much worse. There's so much guilt there, it's incalculable. It makes sense now why she wanted to tell this story, and why she wanted to quit life after it."

"It makes sense to you?" Finley asked, shocked.

"Yeah," Kai said. "Babe, if you got so low that you contemplated—or, God forbid, actually attempted and succeeded at—killing yourself, it would mean I completely let you down."

"But it wouldn't, Kai. You can't control everything."

"It isn't that I think I can control everything, but as your partner, I should be able to see it and lift you up before you got that low. That's my job—to protect you, to rescue you… to take care of you."

Finley listened to what Kai was saying and realized that it was the other half of the "butch" personality that she'd never seen when she'd refused to date butch women. It was the wonderful thing about them, that protective, masculine streak.

"Do you think it's something Legend will ever get over?" she asked.

"I can imagine she's been trying to get past it for the last nine years," Kai said. "Maybe she hoped telling their story would help her do that, but it just made it worse instead."

Finley nodded. "Unintended consequences."

"Yeah…" Kai said, morose.

"Babe, don't let this get you down. You have enough to worry about over there."

Kai laughed softly. She loved that Finley had been able to tell that she was getting mired in Legend's tragedy, even from thousands of miles away on a phone.

"I love you," she said softly.

"I love you, honey," Finley said. "You're starting to sound tired. Go get some sleep, okay?"

"Okay. I'll call you tomorrow."

"Okay, babe. Good night."

Kai lay in her bunk a short while later, thinking about what had happened to Legend, and that it could have just as easily been her. It made her feel so fortunate to have found Finley. She genuinely believed that Fate had given her Finley, and that it was her job to appreciate that gift—and she did, every day, all the time.

Chapter 7

As Legend drove her black Barracuda out of the private parking garage in the hangar area of LAX, Riley sat beside her, wondering how wise it was to let her drive. Legend looked like herself well enough, wearing her faded jeans, black combat boots, and black tank, with a leather-and-sweatshirt hooded jacket and her aviator sunglasses.

Riley had had a service drop her off at the airport when they'd left; she'd been more than happy to call them now, but Legend had refused to leave her car at the airport any longer.

Legend had immediately plugged in her phone, and music flowed from the speakers. The song that came on, however, had Riley cringing. It was "Courtesy Call" from Sixx:A.M.

"I hate this song," she said.

Legend glanced over at her, perplexed. "Why?"

"It's the song that was playing... when I found you. It seemed almost pointed."

"It wasn't, it was just on," Legend said. "You know, I hadn't eaten in two days, so the scotch and pills hit pretty fast."

Riley grimaced painfully. "I don't want to think about that."

"Sorry," Legend said, grimacing too.

She hit the button to change the song, and "Van Nuys" by Sixx:A.M. came on. It had the line "No one wants to die in Van Nuys..."

"No one wants to die in Van Nuys?" Riley asked, thinking it was weirdly specific.

"Yeah, it's why I bought in Malibu," Legend said, grinning.

"That's not funny, Legend."

Legend dropped her head. "I'm sorry. I'm just... I'm sorry."

Riley reached across the seat, touching Legend's hand, her look searching.

"Did you go into making this movie knowing that you wanted to do what you did at the end?" she asked softly.

Legend looked contemplative for a long moment, then shook her head.

"No," she said. "I honestly thought I could tell our story and finally get it out of my head."

"What changed?"

"I had no idea how hard it was going to be to relive all of that again," Legend said, her voice full of emotion. "Eventually I was just praying I could stay alive long enough finish it."

Riley drew in a sharp breath, stunned. "You were hurting that much?" she asked, wondering how she'd missed that.

"Not at first," Legend said softly. "You helped me a lot at first, but things just kept getting worse, and harder, and... closer."

"To the end," Riley said softly.

Legend nodded gravely. "I just wanted it to end."

"Do you still feel that way?" Riley asked, needing to know the answer.

Legend looked pensive, as if she were looking inside herself to see whether she did or didn't. Finally she shrugged, shaking her head. "I don't know."

Riley pressed her lips together, wishing Legend had been able to say a very definite no but happy that she hadn't said yes either. It was a step in the right direction.

They were both silent for a while as Legend got on the 405.

"So, am I dropping you off at home?" she asked, glancing over at Riley.

"Uh, no," Riley said pointedly.

Legend pursed her lips. "So the babysitting will continue, huh?"

"Until I know you're going to be okay, yes."

Legend made a noise in the back of her throat. "That could be a lifetime."

"Is that a proposal?" Riley asked, raising an eyebrow.

"Oh, hell no!"

Riley chuckled at the immediate reaction.

A while later, she glanced over at Legend. "How much do you have at the house?" she asked, not needing to clarify what she meant; Legend knew she was referring to the drugs.

Legend didn't answer at first, her right hand on her thigh rubbing up and down. "The addict in me doesn't want to answer that question," she said eventually.

Riley nodded, understanding that. "But if you start again..."

Legend nodded, looking agitated suddenly. She reached over and turned up the stereo; the song "We Will Not Go Quietly" was on. Legend sang along, moving her head and drumming her fingers on the steering wheel. The bridge fit how Legend seemed to be feeling at that point, since she sang it with zeal. The lyrics talked about blowing it up and giving it hell, but the last line—"You can try to kill yourself, but you can never kill me"—seemed very pointed.

By the time they reached Legend's house in Malibu, it was evident that she was getting tired. Riley had been told by the doctors and by Finley that the withdrawals from speed could last months and would frequently cause extreme fatigue. She helped her up the stairs to her room, helping her take off her boots and her jacket and then putting her in bed. Legend was asleep moments later.

Riley gazed around the room, noticing the artwork. It was all contemporary, with lots of color, depicting trees in huge, sweeping strokes. She had a series of panes over her bed that went from gray, black, and white into rich oranges and fiery reds. It was beautiful. The more she looked around, the more Riley could see the Legend she'd come to know in Rabat, before the sadness and drugs had changed her. It proved to her that the Legend she'd come to know and love was real and existed beyond the addiction and depression.

She called Finley, telling her that they were back and that she was at Legend's house.

"You're staying with her?" Finley asked.

"Yes. The doctors said that her withdrawal symptoms could last a while."

"Weeks, even months, Mom, depending on how long she's been using and how much," Finley said unhappily.

"Would you be willing to come over and check on her? I mean, you know, medically?"

"She should go to a hospital. In fact, she should be in rehab."

"She's not going to do that, Finley. There's no point in even suggesting it."

"You aren't equipped to handle an addict, Mom—you're really not. She needs professional help."

"Well, I'm the only one she's trusting at this point, so I guess I'm it," Riley said sharply.

"I don't like it."

"I can tell. Will you please just come look in on her for me?"

Finley sighed. "Fine, but… Fine."

Riley knew her daughter wasn't happy about her relationship with Legend, and she didn't blame her, really. Finley had been through a number of relationships that Riley hadn't approved of. Basically every relationship she'd had before Kai Temple. Finally, in Kai, Finley had found someone that loved her for her, and took care of her. Riley adored Kai.

The next morning, when Finley arrived at the house, Legend was still asleep.

"She's sleeping a lot," Riley said.

"That's pretty normal," Finley said. "Depression is also highly likely."

Riley nodded. "That's what they told me in Rabat, too. I'm going to go and wake her up."

"Okay."

Riley went into the bedroom. She knelt down next to the bed and reached out to touch Legend on the cheek.

"Legend?" she said softly.

Legend stirred, opening her eyes slowly.

"Finley's here. I asked her to check on you."

Legend blinked a couple of times, rubbing her face on her shoulder, but then nodded.

Riley walked out of the room. "She's awake."

When Finley went to go in, Riley started to follow.

"Mom, let me handle this, okay?" Finley said, holding her hand up.

"Uh…" Riley stammered.

"I'm a doctor. I think I can handle her," Finley said wryly.

"Fine," Riley said, rolling her eyes. "I'll go make some coffee."

When Finley walked into the bedroom, she could see immediately that Legend was still deep in the effects of the withdrawals. She looked exhausted and strained.

Legend moved to sit up, closing her eyes slowly as a wave of dizziness hit her.

"You okay?" Finley asked.

"Yeah, just a bit… off."

Finley pressed her lips together. "Can I have your arm?" she asked, pulling a blood-pressure cuff out of her bag.

Legend put her arm out, leaning against the headboard.

Finley checked her blood pressure, grimacing slightly. "It's still kind of high," she said, giving Legend a pointed look. "Have you used since you've gotten back?"

"No," Legend said evenly.

Finley stared back at the other woman, not sure she believed her. "How much do you have here in the house?" she asked, more sharply than she'd meant to.

Legend looked back at her for a long moment, her lips curling slightly. "You and your mother ask the same questions…"

"Did you answer her?" Finley asked, her eyes narrowed.

This time Legend did grin. "I get it," she said. "You don't want me anywhere near your mother, do you?"

"Not particularly, no."

Legend nodded, her gaze inscrutable.

"I'm sorry," Finley said, shaking her head. "My mother hasn't had a lot of experience with addicts, and I've had far too much, so…"

Legend put her tongue to her teeth, pursing her lips, raising her eyebrows in acknowledgment.

Finley continued her checks, examining Legend's eyes and taking her pulse. She was a bit disconcerted by the fact that Legend wasn't trying to defend herself, or to convince Finley that she wasn't an addict.

"How's the fatigue?" Finley asked.

"It's fun," Legend said sarcastically.

Finley narrowed her eyes. "Are you eating?"

"Sure."

"Any pain or discomfort in your chest?"

Legend stared back at her for a long moment, then shook her head.

"And how are cravings?" Finley asked.

"Oh, they're the best part," Legend said derisively, her eyes, a dark amber color at that point, narrowing.

"If you're not going to answer my questions, I can't help you."

"I don't recall asking for your help."

"No, my mother did for you," Finley snapped.

Legend's eyes widened slightly at Finley's tone, her lips pursed. "Then you don't need to waste your time anymore."

"Legend…" Finley began, starting to feel like she'd overdone it a bit on the judgment.

"Thanks for coming by," Legend said dismissively, her eyes as cold as ice.

Finley swallowed against the lump in her throat. She'd never been so rude to someone she was caring for, and now she felt like shit for doing it. She also knew it was too late to fix it. Getting up, she gave Legend one last look. Legend stared back at her, her gaze assessing, but she didn't say anything else. Finley left the room.

"Is everything okay?" Riley asked, seeing the look on Finley's face.

"Yes," Finley said. "As best I can tell. Her blood pressure is slightly elevated, but that could just be the stress her body is going through in the withdrawals. Otherwise she seems okay." She shook her head. "I'm sorry, Mom. I was kind of an asshole, and I pissed her off."

"Why would you do that?" Riley asked, aghast.

Finley shook her head. "I'm worried about you, and she's the reason. I just… I'm sorry, this was a bad idea," she said, walking to the front door. "I'll send you the name of a doctor here in Malibu, so if she needs medical attention you can call her. I'm too close to this to be objective."

"Finley…"

Finley shook her head. "I gotta go, Mom. I'm sorry."

With that, she left.

When Riley went back into Legend's room, Legend was lying down and appeared to be asleep. She sat down in the chair next to the bed and picked up her book. She wasn't happy about Finley's attitude, but she knew she couldn't change it.

Over the next few days, Legend slept for long periods of time. When she was awake, however, she would lie looking up at the ceiling, her mind miles away. Riley did her best to let her work through whatever she was trying to work through, but she finally felt like she needed to say something. Tula had told her that the first edited version of the movie was done, and she wanted Riley to tell Legend.

Riley had another idea. Sitting next to Legend's bed, she waited until she awoke in the morning. Legend opened her eyes, gold in the morning sunlight.

"What?" she asked, seeing the way Riley was looking at her.

"Why did you change the ending?"

Legend blinked a couple of times, then rubbed her face on her shoulder in agitation. "I thought it would be easier."

"But you told the truth all the way up until that point."

Legend nodded.

"So why wouldn't you want to tell it all?" Riley asked.

Legend shook her head. "I don't think I could handle it."

Riley pressed her lips together, nodding, trying to decide whether to push. "Why did you want to tell this story?" she asked.

"Because I thought she deserved that."

"Then why doesn't she deserve the whole truth being told?"

Legend swallowed convulsively, her lips trembling.

"I know it will be hard for you," Riley said. "But I think Georgette's whole story needs to be told. She lost her life because of Don't Ask, Don't Tell."

"She *took* her life, because of me," Legend said solemnly.

"You're wrong about that," Riley said, shaking her head.

"If she hadn't gotten involved with me, she'd still be alive, Ri."

"If Don't Ask, Don't Tell hadn't been in place, it wouldn't have mattered that she fell in love with you! It would have been okay for you two to be together, and you'd probably be married by now and living happily ever after."

Legend stared back at Riley, surprised. "And you think people need to know what she did to prove that point?" she asked.

"I think people need to know how much their witch hunt affected her," Riley said, nodding. "And I can guarantee you that she's not the only one to have ever done that. I think people need to know the reality of it, how desperate it made people."

Legend looked contemplative again, her eyes still reflecting hesitation. Riley could see that she was thinking about what she'd said, so she left it alone for a while, worried that she'd already pushed her too hard. Legend fell silent then, and Riley let her retreat.

A little while later, Legend got up and took a shower, even sitting out on the back deck of the house for an hour, smoking and drinking coffee. Riley hovered nearby, but tried to leave her alone to think.

Later that evening, Legend was lying on her bed again, having taken a nap. When she woke Riley was in her usual place, reading the paper. Legend lay looking at her, taking in the long dirty-blond hair that was in a ponytail and the blue eyes so much like Georgette's. Then she started to see how tired Riley looked, with dark circles under her eyes. She also started to see how gaunt she was—so she wasn't eating either. It jabbed at her that she hadn't noticed before. Riley was spending all of her time looking after her and not looking after herself. Legend shook her head; Riley caught the movement out of the corner of her eye and looked over.

Without a word, Legend reached out her hand. Riley looked surprised and a bit confused by the gesture, but she took Legend's hand. Legend tugged at her as she shifted backward on the bed to make room. Still looking perplexed, Riley moved to sit on the bed.

"Lay here with me," Legend said, pulling her down.

Riley lay down, searching Legend's face.

Legend reached up, touching Riley's cheek, her expression pained.

"You're here watching me so closely, you're forgetting to look after you."

Riley shook her head. "I'm fine."

"No," Legend said. "You aren't sleeping enough, and I can tell you're not eating either. Isn't that what you were trying to get me to do more of?"

Riley pressed her lips together, looking contrite. "Yes, but…"

"But you weren't taking speed and downers on top of that?" Legend asked, her tone lighter than Riley would have expected.

"Basically," Riley said, smiling softly.

"Yeah, well, I'll make you a deal," Legend said, sounding more like herself suddenly.

"What kind of deal?" Riley asked, her blue eyes twinkling.

"You sleep when I sleep, and you eat when I eat."

Riley smiled. "I think I can make that deal."

"And you sleep here," Legend said, indicating where Riley was lying. "Not in that chair or anywhere else in this house, just with me."

Riley smiled, liking the way Legend had put it. "I think that can be arranged."

Legend smiled too, then laid her hand against Riley's cheek. "I'm sorry I didn't see this sooner," she said, her look pained. "I was too caught up in my own shit…"

"Legend, I'm fine," Riley said. "Don't take this onto yourself too. I've been focused on making sure you're okay, and yeah, I've not been paying too much attention to myself, but that's short term, and it's okay."

"Well, it stops now. You've been paying all this attention to me, and now it's time for me to return the favor."

Riley smiled, hearing the protectiveness in Legend's voice and finding that she really liked it applied to her.

"Is it really crazy that I love the sound of that?" she asked.

Legend's lips curled in a grin. "Well, it wouldn't be if you were gay…"

In response, Riley leaned in and kissed Legend, and was excited to feel her respond instantly. They kissed hungrily for a few minutes, both ending up breathless.

"I'm thinking you might be gay…" Legend said, out of breath, even as she grinned.

Riley smiled. "I'm thinking you might be right."

Remington was out with part of Kai's unit; they were on the opposite side of the town, checking for any new damage or people trapped after the latest round of aftershocks.

"I'm gonna take the dog in here," John Ramis said to Remington, gesturing to a doorway leading into the anteroom of a church.

"Got it," Remington said, turning to look around.

There'd been reports of people starting to loot places like churches, stealing whatever they could sell to get money or supplies. So she was particularly on her guard, her finger to the side of her M16's trigger guard.

"Might have something!" John called. "But I need help moving this bench. Can you help?"

"Yeah," Remington said, moving through the doorway and swinging her rifle to her back.

The two of them shifted the bench, which was lying over a pile of rubble. They didn't notice the piece of wood that was braced against it. As they moved it, the wall John was standing close to started to crumble. Remington dove at him, pushing him forward so that the brick and mortar missed him. Unfortunately it caught Remington with its full weight. Her helmet went skittering across the pavement as she was caught under the debris. John hit the other wall and was unconscious instantly.

Kai hadn't been able to raise Remington or Ramis on the radio, so she was headed down to where they'd been working, doing her best not to completely freak out. They'd been having problems with radios after the last few quakes, so it was possible that theirs just weren't working.

As Kai approached the area, she could hear a dog bark. She whistled and issued the command to come. John Ramis' dog came running from the collapsed church.

"Son of a bitch!" Kai yelled, putting her radio up to her mouth. "Unit Seven, report to the church, east side of town, now! Two soldiers down!"

She rushed into the church, trying to figure out where they could possibly be. She glanced down at the dog she'd been working with. "Sasha, search!"

The tan dog took off immediately, and Kai gave the search command to Rambo, Ramis' dog, as well. She grimaced as she followed them and they both hit on the same area, though she was somewhat relieved when she walked around the partial wall and saw Ramis lying on a pile of rubble. She didn't see Remington, though, and that worried her.

The rest of her unit came on the run. They pulled John out of the debris and two men took him off to the medic. Kai gave Sasha the search command again; this time she hit on the pile of rubble to the right of where John had been.

"Fuck!" Kai yelled, and immediately started shifting bricks and rock. Her unit jumped in to help. "Remi!"

One of the men uncovered a hand, and Kai immediately checked for a pulse—she was relieved to find one.

"Okay, double time, guys!" she said, moving as quickly as she could to heave rubble off her friend.

Within five minutes they were able to uncover Remington. She had a gash on her head and lots of cuts and bruises. She was breathing, but unconscious. They carried her to the medic. An hour later, Kai was waiting nervously for the doctors to let her know Remington's status. She didn't want to call Wynter until she knew something useful.

When the doctor walked out, Kai strode over to him.

"How is she?"

"She has a severe concussion," the doctor said. "We're keeping an eye on her, and she'll need to stay in the hospital for a bit. But she's strong. I'm confident she'll make a full recovery."

Kai breathed a deep sigh of relief, nodding. "Thank you, Doctor."

She pulled out her phone and made the call she'd been dreading since they'd found Remington. She dialed Wynter's number.

Wynter knew something was wrong the moment she saw Kai's name on the display.

"What happened?" she asked as soon as she answered.

"You need to know she's going to be okay."

"Oh Jesus… What happened?"

"A wall collapsed. It looks like she probably shoved one of my guys out of the way—at least, that's what he's saying. She got caught by the debris."

"Always the hero…" Wynter muttered tremulously.

"That's who she is," Kai said, grinning. "Anyway, she's going to be fine. She has a nasty concussion, but the doctors are confident she'll be okay."

"I'm coming there."

"I figured you would," Kai said. "Let me know when you're getting in and I'll pick you up myself."

"Okay, thank you, Kai."

BJ Sparks' personal jet touched down at Ciampino Airport sixteen hours later. Kai waited at the gate, wearing her uniform. She was completely surprised when both Wynter and Finley came through the private terminal gate.

"Oh my God…" Kai had time to say, then Finley ran up and threw herself into her arms, hugging her tight.

"I have missed you so much," Finley said, inhaling the scent of Kai's uniform and soap, and just the scent of *her*, thinking she'd died and gone to heaven.

"Why didn't you tell me you were coming?" Kai said, still holding Finley to her and not caring about the looks people were giving them.

"I wanted to surprise you."

"Well, you succeeded," Kai said as she finally let Finley go and moved to hug Wynter.

"How is she?" Wynter asked.

"Good," Kai said. "Stable."

Wynter took a deep breath and expelled it. She'd been worried that something would have changed in the time it had taken her to get there.

"Come on, we're this way," Kai said, taking Finley's hand and leading them out the side entrance to where the Humvee was parked.

"How far is the hospital?" Wynter asked as they climbed into the vehicle.

"About two hours," Kai said, grimacing. "We're a bit out there."

Wynter nodded, appreciating the fact that Kai had come for her. She knew that if she'd had to figure out how to get there, especially with all the chaos going on in the areas affected by the earthquakes, she would have been lost. Traveling with a military person would be much easier at that point. As they drove through the Italian country-side, Finley looked around excitedly. She'd never taken the time to travel, so had never been anywhere other than the east for college.

They'd been on the road about an hour when the areas affected by the earthquakes started to become apparent. They went through towns where buildings were nothing but rubble.

"Jesus, this is what you guys have been dealing with?" Wynter asked.

"Yeah," Kai said. "We're further north, near Campi, but yeah, pretty much the same level of devastation."

"Wow…" Wynter said, shaking her head.

"Any chance I'll get to see where you guys have been working?" Finley asked.

Kai grinned, glancing over at her. "You came all this way and think I won't show you around a bit?"

"I just didn't know if I'm not allowed or something."

"You're with me—you're allowed."

Another hour later they arrived at the hospital. Kai took them up immediately. Wynter walked over to Remington's bed, grimacing when she saw her. Remington was asleep. There were bruises and cuts on her face, and a bandage on the gash on her head. Wynter sat down, reaching out to touch Remington's face.

Finley went over to the end of the bed and picked up the chart, interested to see if she could read anything on it. Predictably it was in Italian; she did recognize the medications they were giving Remington, though.

"Anything useful?" Kai asked, walking up behind Finley and sliding her arms around her waist.

"She's on some pretty good painkillers," Finley said, grinning and happily leaning back against Kai.

"Oorah," Kai said.

They waited for the doctor to come by. Finley talked to him at length outside the room. When she returned she looked relieved.

"What did he say?" Wynter asked.

"She's doing really good," Finley said. "They're not seeing any signs of brain swelling. She's been awake and fully cognizant. They're watching her for the next couple of days to be safe, since she took such a hard blow, but they're happy with her progress."

Wynter took a deep breath, nodding. If Finley was happy with what she'd been told, then she was happy.

The hospital staff brought Wynter a more comfortable chair and talked excitedly about how brave Remington was to help their people and how wonderful it was that the "US Marines" were there to help the people of Italy.

"Nothing like being appreciated, huh?" Finley said to Kai.

"It's pretty nice, for a change," Kai said. "In the Middle East they liked to treat us like we were invaders. Not all of them, but some."

Finley nodded, still very glad Kai hadn't been deployed back to the Middle East.

"You guys can go if you want," Wynter said. "I'm going to stay here with Remi."

"There's a hotel down the street here," Kai said. "We can get you checked in, in case you want to shower or anything."

"Okay," Wynter said. "Thanks, Kai."

"No problem," Kai said, taking Finley's hand.

They drove over to the hotel, taking in the small bag Wynter had brought with her as well as Finley's.

"We need two rooms," Finley told Kai, her look pointed.

"Uh," Kai stammered, grinning. "Okay."

"I assume there's no room for me where you're staying, so…"

"Well, that's a safe statement. Besides, I'm not letting you sleep where my men are. I'd have to stay up all night to guard you."

"Uh-huh," Finley said. "And if you're gonna stay up all night, I can think of much better things for us to do."

"Can you now?" Kai asked, her dark eyes sparkling.

"Oh yes…" Finley said, sliding her hands inside Kai's uniform jacket.

"Can we at least get to the room first?" Kai asked, seeing the front-desk lady looking at them with interest.

"Spoilsport," Finley said, chuckling.

Twenty minutes later, Kai opened the door to their room; they'd already deposited Wynter's bag in another. Before she could even get the door closed behind them, Finley was kissing her. Kai had to pick Finley up to move her far enough away from the door that she could close it. Finley responded by wrapping her legs around Kai's waist, her lips still on Kai's.

"I'd say you missed me," Kai murmured as she carried her over to the bed.

They spent the next hour thoroughly enjoying each other and doing their best not to be too loud. Afterward they lay under the covers, happy and sated.

"And Cassie is…" Kai said.

"With Xandy and Quinn, as are the boys."

"Oh Lord," Kai said, rolling her eyes.

"I'm sorry," Finley said, sliding her hand over Kai's skin, making Kai shiver in response. "Wynter asked me to come because she said she wanted a doctor she knew to tell her if Remi was really okay. And I really couldn't resist the chance to see you…"

"It's okay," Kai said, smiling. "This was a really nice surprise."

"Do you think they'll send Remi home?"

"I'm recommending it. They said she could experience headaches and issues for another few weeks. I don't want her here trying to deal with that."

Finley nodded. "I don't suppose you could have them send you home too…"

"If it was that easy, I would have already done it."

Finley sighed, nodding.

"I need to get back soon," Kai said, glancing at her watch.

"Can I come with you?"

"Sure," Kai said, smiling. "I'll bring you back here later."

"Can you stay with me later?"

Kai grimaced. "Not sure about that. I have to see where we are there. If I can break away, I will. I promise, okay?"

"Okay."

Finley knew Kai hadn't expected her to be there, so she was willing to take anything she could get. She was actually thrilled they'd had time to make love.

They drove the roads north toward Campi. Finley could see all the debris and crumbled buildings; it was really a lot more scary to be there than just hearing about it.

"God, Kai," she said as she looked out the window of the Humvee. "This is just awful."

"Yeah, some people have lost everything they own," Kai said, turning onto one of the avenues they'd managed to clear of rubble and debris.

"How many people have you managed to pull out though?"

"We're up to about fifty now."

"That's amazing," Finley said, shaking her head.

They pulled up to the building where Kai's office was located. Getting out, Finley followed Kai inside. The building was small, and definitely old, but it was for the most part undamaged. Kai walked her through, having to stop to return a few salutes.

"Scared of you right now," Finley said as they walked through the doors to the suite of offices.

Kai grinned. "Stop it."

"Oh, good, you're back. I need you to sign this, this, and this…" Sands said, her eyes straying over to Finley, who smiled tightly.

"Sands, this is my fiancée, Finley. Fin, this is Lance Corporal Gemma Sands."

"Nice to meet you in person, ma'am," Sands said.

"You too," Finley said, thinking that she'd like to add, *Now keep your hands off my woman,* but she didn't.

Kai raised an eyebrow at Finley's look, but didn't say anything. She knew Finley had seen that Sands was flirting with her a bit, so she figured she was trying to make a point. In Kai's office, Finley sat in the one chair, gazing around.

"Cozy," she said.

"Hey, it works."

Over the next few hours, Finley got to see Kai being the boss. She got to hear a lot of Marine talk, and met a couple of Kai's men. They were all very respectful and polite.

"Wow, I didn't know men could act like that," Finley said, grinning, after the third Marine left.

"They know better around me," Kai said. "I don't put up with disrespect of women, not in my presence."

"And that's part of why I love you."

"Ma'am," Sands said from the doorway.

"Hey," Kai said, smiling as Sands let the leash of the dog Kai had been working with go so she could run over to Kai. "Sasha, you need to meet my other girl," she said, rubbing the dog's head.

"Is this Sasha?" Finley asked, moving to kneel on the floor, turning slightly as she put her hand out to the dog.

Kai smiled. "You remember."

"Of course I remember. That was our first intimate moment together."

Kai laughed. "Uh-huh, my first chance to get close to you…"

Finley glanced up and saw that Sands was still standing in the doorway. "Ostensibly she was protecting me from her dogs," she said with a grin.

Sands widened her eyes. "But really…?" she asked, looking at Kai.

"But really I'd been dying to get next to her for about a week and a half."

Finley laughed. "Right, since I'd met you in the emergency room of the hospital and I had to take out your appendix."

"You met in the emergency room?" Sands asked.

"Fin was my doctor," Kai said, grinning as Sasha rolled onto her back to beg Finley to scratch her belly, which she promptly did.

"Wow." Sands looked surprised. "I actually thought you were a movie star."

"No, that's my mom."

Sands looked at both of them to see if Finley was joking.

"Her mom is Riley Taylor," Kai said, winking at Finley.

"Oh my God, I love her!" Sands said.

"How's Legend doing, by the way?" Kai asked.

Finley nodded. "Sounds like she's doing good."

"So, maybe out of the woods?"

"Maybe," Finley said, knowing that Kai was really rooting for Legend Azaria to come through her recent trauma.

"Are you talking about Legend Azaria, that director?" Sands asked.

"Yeah," Finley said, glancing at Kai.

Sands grinned. "She's really hot."

Kai laughed, shaking her head. "Not my type at all."

"She's pretty hot," Finley said.

"I see…" Kai said, giving her a narrowed look.

"Hey, I can look, I just can't touch."

Kai canted her head. "Who said that? And since when are you into butches?"

Finley laughed. "I believe I'm wearing your ring…"

"I believe I didn't give you a choice about that…"

Finley just smiled widely.

Later that afternoon, Kai showed her around the area they'd been working. Finley was surprised that Kai carried an M16 as they walked around.

"Do you usually carry that?" she asked.

"Yeah, just not at the ready if I have Sasha with me."

"Why?"

"I need my hands free to direct her."

"I gotta say, the rifle thing is kinda sexy..."

Kai laughed. "Is there anything about the Marine thing you don't find sexy?"

"Yes, the possibility of you getting hurt," Finley said, smiling sweetly.

"Oh," Kai said, nodding.

It was almost nine o'clock by the time Kai was able to free herself up enough to go back to the hotel with Finley. They had a nice meal at the restaurant and indulged in hours of lovemaking, which Kai knew she'd regret the next day when she'd be exhausted, but it was worth it.

Wynter was reading a book she'd brought with her when Remington woke up.

"You're here," Remington said.

"Of course I'm here," Wynter said, leaning over Remington and kissing her softly. "BJ loaned me his plane and pilot."

"Gotta love that guy..."

"I do," Wynter said. "How do you feel?"

"My head hurts."

"That's 'cause a building fell on it, babe."

"Is Ramis okay?"

Wynter gave a short laugh, shaking her head. "Always worried about everyone else... Yes, he's fine, and you are being credited with saving his ass."

"Rambo okay too?"

"Yes, the dog is fine too," Wynter said, her look pointed. "Gonna ask how you are?"

"I know I'm okay," Remington said, smiling softly.

"How?"

"Because you're perfectly calm. And you wouldn't be if you were worried about me."

"Oh, I'm worried about you, but I brought my own doctor, who told me you're just fine, so..."

Remington grinned. "You brought Fin?"

"Yep," Wynter said, smiling.

"But no Memphis?"

"She's knee-deep in the soundtrack of *For the Telling* right now—I didn't want to drag her away. She sends her love, though, and wants you to get your ass home now."

"Well, she's gonna get her wish. Kai's having me sent home."

"Really?" Wynter asked, looking surprised but thrilled at the same time.

Remington nodded. "Thought you might like that."

"Oh, I love that… and you," Wynter said, moving to kiss Remington again.

The morning after her conversation with Riley, Legend woke and curled her arms around her, pulling her closer. Riley was awake, and turned over.

"Good morning," she said, smiling.

"Morning," Legend said, smiling too. "I've made a decision."

"About?"

"The movie. I'm going to reshoot the ending."

Riley bit her lip, her eyes shining as she nodded.

"I'm gonna need you, though…" Legend said.

Riley grinned. "Well, yeah…"

"No, I mean I'm going to need you to help me through it… like you did before."

"I'll be right here, right by your side the whole time."

"That's what I was hoping you'd say," Legend said softly.

Later that week, on a sound stage in Hollywood, the cast and crew gathered to receive the pages for the new ending. Before she had them handed out, Legend stood before all of them.

"As some of you may know, or may have guessed, this project is very near and dear to me. It's probably a little too near and dear to me," she said, looking at Riley, her expression pained. "Georgette Teresa Griffin was a real person, and she was the woman I was in love with my last year in the Marines, when I was stationed in the Middle

East. Everything you've filmed thus far has been as true to real life as I could make it. It's our story. As some of you may or may not know, the last day of filming was a bit... much for me... and I tried to take my own life that day. I'm hoping that's something that can stay between all of us, but do with it what you will. It's the truth. It's what this kind of thing can do to you."

There were nods, looks of surprise, and a lot of concerned glances. Legend took them in and nodded, her emotions clear.

"What wasn't real was the last scene," she said, nodding to the assistants to start passing out the new pages. "What you're getting now is what really happened. And it's how we're now going to end the movie."

Everyone began reading the new pages immediately. There were sniffles and tears from many of the cast and crew as they learned the truth about what had happened. Riley walked over to Legend, putting her hand to her back, feeling that she was trembling as she watched people's reactions. Legend could see how affected people were by the information they'd just received, and she could hear people murmuring about how much DADT sucked and how this just wasn't right. It strengthened her resolve to tell the story the right way.

She turned to Riley, looking into her eyes.

"Looks like you were right," she said.

Riley nodded. "Are you okay?"

Legend took a deep breath, expelling it slowly. "No, not really. But I will be."

Riley nodded, appreciating that Legend wasn't candy-coating it.

"You ready to do this?" Legend asked.

"As ready as I'm ever going to be."

When Legend called cut, there wasn't a dry eye in the place. Riley could see that she was feeling the effects of the scene, but was valiantly holding it together. After everyone left, Riley checked on her.

"How are you?" she asked.

Legend drew in a deep breath, blowing it out as she nodded slowly.

"Want to go get some dinner?" Riley asked.

Legend grinned. "I want a steak. A serious steak."

They went to Morton's Steakhouse on La Cienega Boulevard. The paparazzi had a field day with the ever-controversial Legend Azaria having dinner with her latest leading lady, the extremely famous and talented Riley Taylor. They asked all kinds of questions, none of which either Riley or Legend answered. Inside they knew they were being observed, and Riley found that she didn't really care. She reached over, taking Legend's hand in hers.

Legend could hear the paparazzi's cameras clicking away. "You do realize that picture will be all over the place by morning."

Riley grinned. "You think so?"

Legend licked her lips, shaking her head, her eyes gold in the candlelight.

"What do you think will happen with this?" Riley asked, leaning across the table to kiss Legend softly on the lips, then pulling back to look into her eyes.

"I think you just came out and your publicist is going to kill you," Legend said, smiling broadly.

That was the picture on the front page of every tabloid paper the next morning.

Chapter 8

Finley kissed Kai goodbye, hugging her tight.

"Please, please be careful," Finley said against Kai's uniform shirt.

"I will be, honey. I promise."

Kai turned to Remington, extending her hand. "You take it easy back home for a bit, huh?"

"I think Wynter plans on it," Remington said.

"Damned right I do," Wynter said, nodding vehemently.

A little while later, the three boarded BJ's plane. Kai watched them take off, then turned and went back to the Humvee.

Legend stepped into the sound booth, looking over at Memphis. Memphis glanced up, her eyes widening.

"Hi," Memphis said, clearly surprised.

"Sorry, I've kind of sucked at being useful," Legend said, sitting down at the soundboard next to her.

"You were dealing with a lot. I get that."

Legend nodded, having heard about Memphis' childhood and more recent trauma.

"Can I hear what you have?" she asked.

"Sure," Memphis said, and cued up the music for the soundtrack that she'd been working on.

Two hours later, Legend was beyond ecstatic that she'd hired someone as talented as Memphis Lassiter.

"You completely nailed it," she said, her eyes bright and slightly awed. "Somehow you caught everything I wanted, without even talking to me."

"I was getting the dailies as they were coming through," Memphis said. "I got the feel for it from those."

"This is completely amazing, Memphis... I don't even know where to begin."

Memphis smiled. "I had a blast working on it."

"Well, I think we'll need to work together again, then."

"I'm there—you just tell me when."

Legend drove back to Malibu feeling completely unbreakable. At the house she noted that Riley's car was there, which meant she'd gone to her house and still come back. She walked inside and saw Riley out on the back porch. Going out, she took Riley into her arms and kissed her deeply.

"I take it the sound session went well?" Riley asked.

"Memphis Lassiter is a genius!" Legend said. "She nailed everything I wanted and some stuff I didn't even realize I wanted."

"Wow," Riley said, smiling brightly. "I'm really glad."

Legend nodded, taking a deep breath and blowing it out. "Editing is almost done. I need to check it out again, and I need to get a premiere scheduled."

"Seems like it."

"You know," Legend said, "I will need a date for that…" She let her voice trail off as she looked up.

"You will, huh?" Riley asked, narrowing her eyes. "Are you asking me to be your date?"

"I'm definitely asking you to be my date."

Riley smiled. "Then I'm definitely accepting."

"That's handy," Legend said, just as her phone started ringing.

She pulled it out and looked at the display, not recognizing the number. She answered it anyway. Riley could only hear Legend's side of the conversation.

"Hello?" Legend blinked. "Yes, this is Legend Azaria—who's this?"

Riley became alarmed when Legend just about dropped her phone as she staggered slightly. Riley immediately moved her to a chair on the patio.

"I… Yes—yes, sir," Legend said, nodding. "I… Well… Yes." She closed her eyes slowly, and Riley watched as a tear slid down her cheek.

Riley knelt in front of Legend, her hands on her legs, looking up at her. Legend opened her eyes and stared down at Riley, her expression beatific.

"Yes, sir, I do… No, sir, I didn't know that… Yes, I did." Legend's eyes widened. "Of course, sir, of course. You just tell me how many you need." Again her eyes widened. "Okay, yes, of course I can." Legend listened for another minute, then closed her eyes slowly, tears sliding from them again. "No, sir, I had no idea. Okay, that would be… Yes. Okay… Yes, I'd like that. If you send me the address I can get them to you as soon as we set a date… I will… Thank you, sir. You too. Goodbye."

Legend hung up and set the phone on the table in front of her, looking completely shell-shocked.

"What was that about?" Riley asked, worried.

"That," Legend said, looking down at her, "was Georgette's father. He said he was contacted by Riley Taylor…"

Riley grimaced. "I sent him a letter. I just told him that I knew a friend of his daughter's and that she was making a movie about her time in the military. He never responded, so I didn't want to say anything to you."

"Well, that was him, so you must have given him my cell phone?"

Riley bit her lip. "I figured if he wanted to reach out…" she said, hoping Legend wasn't annoyed.

"They want to come to the premiere," Legend said.

"They?"

"Her whole family." Legend looked overwhelmed. "Twenty of them."

"Oh my God!"

"He knows who I am."

"What do you mean?" Riley asked. The look in Legend's eyes told her she didn't just mean by way of what she'd sent him.

"I mean, he knows exactly who I am. Georgette apparently wrote them about me."

"*Everything* about you?"

"She told them she was in love with me…" Legend said, tears in her eyes again.

Riley moved to hug her then, tears in her eyes as well. Legend wrapped her arms around Riley, pulling her down onto her lap and putting her head against Riley's chest. They stayed that way for a long time.

After a while, Riley got up and took Legend's hand, leading her into the house and up to her room. There she took Legend's jacket off, set it aside, and pushed her into a sitting position on the bed so she could untie her combat boots and put them aside as well. She took off her shoes, then sat down, pulling Legend back into her arms. Legend lay against her, her arms around Riley's waist. They fell asleep that way.

Legend woke up at midnight, gripped with the intense desire to take a pill. Her mind told her exactly where to find it, how it would feel, how good it would feel… She fought the desire. Her mind had already started churning. Georgette's family… Her father… The Bible bangers… *Take the pill!* screamed every cell in her body. *Take it now, you won't care about any of this anymore, just take it!*

The screaming in her head drove her to her feet. Riley was still asleep. *Good*, her mind said. *Then she won't see you do it… She won't stop you.*

Legend gritted her teeth, closing her eyes and breathing out slowly. She went over to her bureau and picked up her phone and headphones. Plugging the headphones in, she blasted music into her head, trying to shut that damned voice up. She went downstairs. Her mind was kind enough to remind her where every single stash of pills was along the way. It drove her outside, down to the sand. Still her mind wouldn't stop. Her body was craving the drug in the worst way. Her body wanted her to go back inside, take a pill, let it help her… *Just do it!* her head screamed at her.

Giving a yell, Legend began running at top speed down the beach. She ran and ran, doing everything to shove the desire for drugs out of her head. She barely felt it when the broken bottle sliced her foot open; still she kept running. It was forty degrees and windy on the beach and she was wearing jeans and a tank top; she didn't even feel the cold. By the time she got back to the house she was drenched with sweat, her body shaking from the cold and the incredible desire for speed. Music was still pounding in her head.

She sat down on one of the deckchairs, spreading her legs wide and bending over at the waist, trying to fight the desire to use. Her muscles were tense and screaming at her from the abuse they'd just taken. She looked down at her foot, seeing the blood and staring at it in fascination, welcoming the distraction.

Riley woke and realized Legend wasn't in bed. She checked the bathroom and then saw that Legend's phone and headphones were gone. Pulling on her shoes and jacket, she went downstairs. The back slider to the house was open, and Riley saw Legend sitting in one of the deckchairs. She was relieved, but then saw that Legend wasn't wearing a jacket or even shoes. She also saw the way she was bent over and that her entire body was shaking.

"Legend!" she exclaimed as she walked outside, kneeling in front of her and putting her hands on Legend's—they were like ice. "Come inside, babe, please."

Legend was shaking from head to toe, but she shook her head.

"Please, babe," Riley said, getting up and tugging at Legend to get her to stand.

Legend finally stood, and Riley led her inside, immediately grabbing a blanket to throw around her. They walked over to the couch and Riley sat her down, then went to turn the heater up. She knelt next to the couch. Legend was lying curled almost into a fetal position with her head on the arm of the couch. She was still shaking terribly.

Riley stroked Legend's hair back. "What's going on?" she asked. "Can you tell me?"

Legend shook her head, swallowing convulsively, closing her eyes slowly then opening them again.

Riley searched her face. "Please tell me what's happening."

"Body screaming…" Legend gritted out.

"For the drugs?"

Legend nodded, her body shuddering. She groaned, her entire body contracting in what looked like pain.

Riley stood up and pulled out her phone. Walking over to the kitchen area, she called Finley, keeping her eye on Legend the entire time.

Finley was just finishing her shift at the hospital when her phone rang. She saw that it was her mother and wondered remotely if this was going to be the call to say that Legend had actually managed to overdose and die this time.

"Hey, Mom, what's up?" Finley said as she walked to the parking garage.

"I need your help," Riley said immediately.

"With what?" Finley asked as she reached Kai's Navigator,

216

which she'd been driving while Kai had been gone.

"It's Legend—she's shaking horribly, she's acting like she's in pain. She said her body is screaming for drugs. I don't know what to do."

Finley took a deep breath, blowing it out. "She's probably still having withdrawals—this is just a bad episode. Did she take anything already?" Finley asked, getting into the vehicle and starting it up, the Bluetooth taking over so she could set her phone down.

"I don't think so," Riley said, hearing Legend groan again. "I found her outside. It looks like she'd been running again, but her feet were bare and she's not wearing a jacket. I think she was trying to keep from using."

Finley nodded. "Okay, Mom, I'm gonna come there and give her a sedative. Try to keep her as calm as you can, and don't let her out of your sight. Right now, if she uses she's likely to overdose, so don't let her get away from you, okay?"

"Okay," Riley said. "Please drive carefully."

Finley chuckled. "I'm driving Kai's tank—can't get much more careful than that."

They hung up a minute later, and Riley went back over to the couch, sitting down on the floor in front of Legend. She settled the blanket over her, trying to warm her up. Legend was still shaking, her breathing labored, peppered with slight moans and gasps as her body contracted or shuddered.

"God…" Legend moaned, grimacing in pain, biting her lip and closing her eyes.

"Just hold on, babe," Riley said. "Finley's coming to help."

"You called Finley?" Legend groaned. "She already hates me—now she's going to get to see this. Great..."

"You need help right now. I called her because she can help."

Legend drew in a deep breath, shaking her head, as another shudder ran through her.

Riley spent the next hour talking to Legend, stroking her hair, telling her to just hold on. At one point, Legend started to panic as the pain started all over her body.

"Talk to me," Riley said. "Just talk to me."

Legend moaned out loud. "They're coming to the movie... What if... I can't... What if they... I can't... Oh God... I can't..."

"It'll be okay, babe, it'll be okay," Riley said. "You made a brilliant movie and they're going to see that. They're going to see how much you loved her. It'll be okay."

It was the longest hour of Riley's life. Tula had awakened, as if sensing she was needed, and come out of her room. Riley asked her to watch for Finley.

When Finley arrived, she saw her mother sitting on the floor, one hand stroking Legend's hair, the other rubbing her arm, her eyes intent on Legend's face. She was talking to her, telling her that she would be okay, that help was coming. It struck Finley in that moment that her mother was in love with Legend Azaria, and it made her more determined to help.

"So, party in Malibu tonight, huh?" Finley said, smiling as she walked over to them.

Legend made a noise in the back of her throat that sounded like a chuckle. "You know us Hollywood types..." she said, her voice tremulous and punctuated by gasps.

Finley set her bag down, kneeling to take a look at Legend.

"I'm going to help, okay?" she said gently, reaching out to touch Legend's neck to feel her pulse; it was definitely racing. "Legend, I need you to be totally honest with me right now, okay? Have you taken anything?"

Legend shook her head. "That seems to be the problem at the moment," she gasped out, her mouth tightening as she was wracked with another shudder.

Finley nodded. "I'm going to give you a sedative that should help calm everything down."

Legend nodded, squeezing her eyes shut as she felt another pain rip through her.

"I know it feels like your body is splitting apart, but I promise you, it's not," Finley said as she drew the sedative into the needle. "It's just your mind trying to force the issue. You just keep telling it no and we'll get you through this, okay?"

Legend nodded again, shuddering. Riley put her hand to Legend's cheek, and her forehead to Legend's.

"Just hold on, okay?" Riley told Legend, her voice a soft entreaty. "Just stay with me here."

Legend nodded, her lips trembling with the effort not to scream. She reached up, touching Riley's hand, grasping it.

"Okay, just hold on," Finley said, swabbing a spot on Legend's arm then inserting the needle and pushing the plunger down slowly, glancing over at Legend as she did. "This is going to help, I promise, but you need to try to relax a bit so it can get in, okay?

Legend blew her breath out in a ragged sigh. Finley removed the needle and stuck a small Band-Aid over the injection site. She slid her hand over Legend's arm soothingly.

"Try to relax," she said. "Just let the sedative do its job, it's going to help."

Between Riley's and Finley's voices and their hands smoothing over her skin and squeezing her hand gently, Legend couldn't help but relax. She started to breathe easier as the pain lessened.

"Uh, you do realize your foot is bleeding, right?" Finley asked, humor in her voice.

Legend nodded. "Bottle on the beach—damned tourists," she muttered.

Finley laughed softly. "Well, since I'm here, I'll fix that too."

Finley cleaned the cut and used butterfly closures instead of stitching, not wanting to cause Legend any extra pain at that point. She then bandaged the foot. Legend's eyes were closing by that time, the sedative taking effect.

Riley took Finley's hand, squeezing it gently as she mouthed, "Thank you." Finley nodded, smiling softly at her mother.

They spent the rest of the night watching Legend. She settled more comfortably on the couch, pulling at Riley at one point. Riley smiled as she lay down in front of Legend, who slid her arms around her, snuggling against her and falling asleep again. Finley moved to the other couch, lying down under the blanket there as she texted Cassiana to let her know where she was.

The next morning, Legend lay looking at Riley, who'd turned over during the night to face her. Legend reached up, touching Riley's cheek, smoothing her thumb over her skin. Riley stirred and woke up, looking at Legend, whose eyes were almost gold in the sunlight coming in the windows.

"How are you feeling?" Riley asked softly.

"Hungover," Legend said, closing her eyes slowly then opening them again to look at her. "And again you save me…"

Riley simply smiled softly. After a long moment, Legend looked over to where Finley slept on the other couch. Riley glanced over her shoulder at her daughter, smiling, then turned back to Legend.

"It isn't that Finley doesn't like you, Legend," she said.

"It's that she doesn't like me with you," Legend said, nodding. "I get that. I wouldn't want anyone I loved within a hundred feet of someone like me."

"Someone like you?"

"An addict."

"You're not an addict."

Legend gave a short, humorless laugh. "Last night should have proven to you that I'm an addict, Ri."

"It proved to me that the phone call from her parents really shook you up again."

"It also proved that my body craves drugs when it's stressed out."

Riley pressed her lips together, nodding. "Okay, but I think that last night also proved that you're getting better. Would you have resisted using that much before?"

Legend thought about the question, then shook her head. "No,"

221

she said confidently. "I just didn't want to let you down. You've done so much to try to get me back to good."

"And I'll keep doing that if you let me."

"Aren't you going to want your own life back at some point, babe?"

Riley didn't answer, dropping her eyes to the dog tag that Legend wore. It was flipped over, so the initials showed. Riley reached up, touching the letters engraved there.

"G.T.G.," she said, looking up at Legend.

"Georgette Teresa Griffin," Legend said, her eyes flickering with pain.

Riley nodded sadly.

"I never got to say goodbye to her," Legend said, her eyes taking on a faraway look. "The MPs had followed me to the shed—they were only a minute or two behind me. They took her body out of my arms and took her back to base. By the time I got back, they wouldn't let me see her. They sent her body home to her parents. I don't even know where she's buried…" Her voice trailed off as her eyes glazed with tears.

"So you wear her memorial here," Riley said, touching the tag again.

Legend nodded, her lips trembling slightly as she blew her breath out slowly.

Riley looked up at Legend again. "The movie you made is amazing, Legend, and her family is either going to accept who she was with you or they're not—you can't do anything about that. If they watch it with open hearts, they'll see how much you loved her and how much she loved you in return."

Legend nodded again, looking choked up. "I'm gonna go take a shower," she said. "I need to soak my muscles—they're all killing me this morning."

Riley smiled. "Okay. Just be careful, please. I'm betting that sedative hasn't worn completely off, and I don't want you falling or anything."

Legend grinned. "Well, that would be a whole new set of issues, wouldn't it?"

"Yeah, so let's not, okay?" Riley said, chuckling.

"Okay," Legend said, and leaned in to kiss her softly.

She got up and headed upstairs, limping due to the bandage on her foot. Riley watched her go, her expression fond. Finley, who'd been awake since she'd heard her name and heard them talking, saw the look on her mother's face.

"You're in love with her," Finley said.

Riley glanced over at her daughter, her expression thoughtful, then nodded. Finley nodded too.

"Sounds like she's still really going through it with what happened before," Finley said as she sat up.

"Well, it got stirred up again yesterday. Georgette's father called her."

"I didn't know she knew them."

"She doesn't," Riley said. "I wrote them a letter, telling them about the movie. But apparently I wasn't the first one to write them about Legend—Georgette had too."

"Legend didn't know that?"

"No. Georgette had told her that her family were all Bible bangers and they'd flip completely out if she was gay."

"The guy didn't flip out on her, did he?" Finley asked.

Riley saw the look of anger on her daughter's face and took heart in that.

"No," she said, shaking her head. "They want to come to the premiere of the movie."

Finley looked surprised. "Really?"

Riley nodded. "And apparently that," Riley said, gesturing toward the stairs, "was about worrying how they'd react to the movie."

Finley nodded slowly. "Makes sense. It is good that she fought taking the pills so hard, Mom. It shows that she's really committed to not using—it's a really good sign."

Riley bit her lip, smiling. "I'm glad."

"You know," Finley said. "It might be a good idea to get her together with Kai when she gets back."

"Why?"

"Maybe Kai can help her get on a healthier track, like she did for you and me. It might help her fight the desire some more too. It might also be good if you two start hanging out with the group more…"

"Sweetie, I don't know that we'll be together after this movie premieres," Riley said sadly.

Finley grimaced. "You think she'll move on?"

Riley shrugged, shaking her head. "I really don't know."

"And that's okay with you?"

Riley took a deep breath, blowing it out slowly. "No," she said. "But I think I really don't have a choice here. I'm here as long as she lets me be."

Finley stared back at her mother. This was not the woman she knew. Her mother was the love-them-and-leave-them one. She'd never been on the other end of that equation. Finley didn't like it at all, and she liked it even less that her mother seemed to be willing to accept whatever happened. She talked to Kai about it later that day.

"It's like she's willing to take whatever Legend gives her," Finley said, sounding sickened at the thought.

"I know that feeling," Kai said.

"What does that mean?"

"Well, that's how I felt with you."

"Until you didn't," Finley said, remembering the way Kai had turned cold on her when she'd been against the idea of moving in with her.

Kai gave a short laugh. "Yeah? And how hard was it to get me back?"

Finley bit her lip. "Not too hard."

"Not too hard at all. I was in love with you, Fin, and I was willing to take whatever you'd give me to keep you."

"I recall someone telling me she wasn't giving me a choice about marrying her when she got back…" Finley said, glancing down at the ring on her finger.

"That's 'cause I have you now, and I know you love me."

Finley sighed. "I wish Legend would see what my mom's going through."

"You don't know that she doesn't, babe. It's not that easy to let yourself fall again, not when the first time went so horribly wrong. Especially in her case."

Finley nodded. "That's true, and she's still really affected by Georgette's death."

"And you said Georgette's family reached out to Legend?"

"Yeah. It really threw her."

"But she didn't use."

"No, and I heard her tell my mom that she normally wouldn't have resisted that hard, but she didn't want to let my mom down, after what she'd done for her."

Kai grinned. "And you think Legend isn't in love with your mother?"

"I…" Finley started. "Jesus…" she breathed. "She is, isn't she?"

"I'd put my money on it, yeah," Kai said. "But either she's fighting it, or she doesn't realize it yet herself. Kinda like someone I know…"

"Yeah, yeah," Finley said, having been the one that had been too afraid to fall for Kai and admit that she loved her.

"Things are going to go the way they're meant to—you know that."

"I know," Finley said. "But I just don't want to see my mom get hurt."

Kai smiled. Finley's attitude toward her mother had changed so much over the last year. When Kai had met Finley and then her mother, Finley had barely put up with her mom. The two would constantly verbally spar. Kai had pointed out to Finley that her mother liked to push her buttons, and when Finley reacted, Riley would push them even more. She'd gotten Finley to stop responding, and the relationship had started improving immediately. They'd learned how to treat each other better, and they'd grown closer because of that.

"We'll just have to see what happens, honey," Kai said, smiling.

"I know," Finley said. "I miss you."

"I miss you."

"Can you come home now?"

"I wish, baby," Kai said softly.

"Okay," Finley said, sounding very young suddenly. "I love you."

"I love you too."

They hung up a short while later.

After Finley left the house in Malibu, Riley went upstairs to check on Legend. She was just drying off after her shower. Riley surveyed Legend's body. She was very slim, with leanly muscled arms and legs, but her hip bones were apparent and Riley could see the outline of her ribcage.

"We need to make sure you eat more," Riley observed.

Legend grinned. "I've always had a fast metabolism."

"Yeah, but if you eat right, some of the food will actually stick," Riley said, poking her playfully in the ribs.

Legend laughed, grabbing her around the waist and pulling her close. She leaned in and kissed her. The kiss unexpectedly turned heated as Riley slid her arms up around Legend's neck, pressing closer.

Legend tightened her arms around Riley, deepening the kiss and feeling her body shudder—it tripped her libido immediately. Moving her hands to the buttons of Riley's shirt, she made quick work of unbuttoning it, sliding her hands over Riley's skin sensually. Riley moaned softly against Legend's lips, grasping at her head and neck, trying to pull her closer. Minutes later, Legend had Riley naked and against the bathroom counter, pressing tight, moving rhythmically against Riley's body as they both gasped and moaned in their need. Legend's mouth moved over Riley's neck, sucking and biting at her skin as she pressed harder and closer, making Riley gasp loudly as she lifted one leg to wrap around Legend's body. That was the extra contact they both needed, and they both cried out in their release, grasping at each other and riding the wave of intense sensations coursing through them.

Afterward, Legend leaned against Riley, her arms around her, her head against her shoulder, as she did her best to catch her breath. She grinned against Riley's skin, kissing her.

"Now, this is a drug I could get really hooked on…" Legend said huskily.

Riley wrapped her arms around Legend's neck, lowering her head to kiss her shoulder.

"Me too," she said, smiling.

Two weeks later, Finley was in Natalia's class, doing her best to keep up. She'd been doing everything she could think of to avoid thinking about Kai being stuck in Italy. It was almost Thanksgiving, and the thought of not having Kai there broke her heart. She'd already invited everyone in the group to the house for the holiday, determined to do it for Cassiana if nothing else. The girl had had so few normal holidays that Finley wanted to give her that.

Cassiana had missed Kai. She'd talked to her online as much as possible, but it wasn't the same. Finley had considered taking her to Italy when she'd gone with Wynter, but she'd been afraid she'd be putting her in harm's way, so she'd decided against it.

They were just taking a break from the class and Finley was drinking water when she glanced up. Standing there in her uniform was Kai, smiling at her.

"Oh my God!" Finley exclaimed, dropping her water bottle and running to Kai, jumping into her arms as many of the women in the room cheered or clapped.

"Hi, honey, I'm home," Kai said in her ear.

Finley kissed Kai over and over again, her arms and legs wrapped tightly around her. Even so, Kai was able to shake hands with most of the bois standing there, grinning at the fact that Finley was pointedly not letting her go.

"So I guess you're done with class, eh?" Natalia asked Finley as she leaned up to hug Kai, kissing her on the cheek.

"Yeah, I'm gonna go home with my soldier now," Finley said, smiling brightly.

Two days later, Thanksgiving dinner was held at Kai and Finley's house as planned. It was a much more joyous occasion, because now both Kai and Remington were home. Remington had fully re-covered from the concussion and was back to her usual self, including the red tips on her cornrows.

Finley had pointedly invited her mother and Legend, and had been happy when they accepted. They arrived in Legend's Barracuda, which had Remington, Quinn, and half the other bois outside looking at the car.

"This is a thing, huh?" Riley asked Finley as she walked into the house.

"The bois and their cars," Xandy said, smiling. "Oh yes."

"How are things, Mom?" Finley asked.

"Good."

"Legend's doing okay?"

"Yes, no more issues like that last one," Riley said. "In fact, tomorrow we're meeting Georgette's father and mother for lunch."

"Wow. Really?"

"Georgette is the character you played, right?" Wynter asked.

Riley nodded. "Yes."

"And the girl who died," Finley said.

"Oh…" Cat said, grimacing. "That's gotta be rough."

"It was, trust me," Riley said.

"But she's off the stuff now, right?" Cat asked.

"Yes, completely," Riley assured her; she knew about Cat's background in law enforcement.

Cat nodded, looking happy about that. "Jovina said you guys made a hell of a movie."

"You're coming to the premiere, aren't you? All of you?" Riley asked, gesturing to all of the women in the room.

"I think most if not all of us, yeah," Kashena said. She smiled. "We gotta support our own."

"Double meaning there," Sierra said. "Kash was a Marine too."

"I see," Riley said, smiling.

The bois came back into the house then, in the middle of a debate about torque versus horsepower. Finley shook her head as Kai walked over and leaned down to kiss her.

"See? This is what I don't get," Wynter said, shaking her head.

"What don't you get, bebe?" Remington asked.

"Horsepower, smorsepower. Is it pretty? Yes. Does it go fast when I press the gas pedal? Yes. Then drive it—sheesh!"

That had all the bois laughing, and some of the other women as well.

It was a fun evening. Legend found herself included with the group in every conversation. At one point she walked to the far edge of the property, looking out over the canyon as she smoked. Riley joined her.

"You okay?" she asked, sliding her arms around Legend from behind, putting her head to her back.

"Yeah," Legend said, taking a long drag. "Just getting a little edgy about tomorrow."

Riley nodded. "I understand that," she said, flattening her hands against Legend's abdomen. "If it's bad we'll just leave."

Legend blew out a long stream of smoke, nodding pensively.

"Why do you think he wants to meet ahead of time?" she asked.

Riley went around to stand in front of Legend, looking up at her and seeing the worry in her eyes. "Well, he probably figures you're going to be a bit busy the night of the premiere, so he wants to get a chance to talk to you beforehand."

Legend looked down at her, searching Riley's eyes. "You think that's all?" she asked, sounding as worried as she looked.

"I do."

"What if he's planning on giving me some kind of sermon about how being gay is a sin and blah, blah, blah…"

"Then we're leaving," Riley said simply.

Legend pressed her lips together, and Riley knew that she was really hoping that wasn't going to be the case. Riley herself was hoping for the best, that Legend could get some kind of closure with Georgette's family, and maybe with Georgette's death as well.

The next morning, Legend and Riley got up and had coffee. Legend had talked to Kai the night before, and after the premiere she was planning on starting to do some training with her, to work on strengthening her health and endurance so making movies and being completely obsessive wouldn't push her to drugs anymore. It was a step in the right direction.

Three hours later, they walked into The Ivy, with its rustic arched doorways and random vintage furniture and decor. Legend wore black slacks and a short-sleeved gray button-up shirt, and her usual thick black leather watch, combat boots, and leather-and-sweatshirt-style hooded jacket. The dog tag she always wore was in place, as were her aviator sunglasses. Her hair was styled in its usual odd angle, the sides shaved very short. She looked much healthier than she had a month and a half before, in Rabat. Riley was very casual in a cream sweater and blue jeans with ivory boots. Her makeup was light, but as usual made her look like the softly beautiful movie star that she was.

Mr. and Mrs. Griffin were already seated, and the waitress, who knew both Legend and Riley, showed them to the table. Legend squeezed Riley's hand gently as they walked up; Riley squeezed back. Legend extended her hand to Mr. Griffin. He was an older man, with brown hair that was graying at the temples. He was tall and thin, with hands that suggested he worked outdoors. He stood up, taking Legend's hand and shaking it.

"I'm Legend Azaria," she said as she reached up with her other hand to take off her sunglasses.

"George Griffin. This is my wife, Teresa."

"Ma'am," Legend said, nodding to Georgette's mother, then grinning softly. "Guess I know where she got her name. This is Riley Taylor," she said, stepping aside for Riley.

"We know who you are," Teresa said bashfully. "We've seen all of your movies, and we always root for you during the Academy Awards."

Riley smiled brilliantly, her blue eyes sparkling. "Well, thank you," she said. "That's very sweet."

"Please," George said, gesturing for Legend and Riley to sit down.

Legend held Riley's chair for her, then took off her jacket and hung it on the back of her chair before sitting down herself. George's eyes took in the gesture, and he glanced at his wife. Legend's tattoos were on full display now.

"I know this must be really awkward for you," George said, his blue eyes, the same color as Georgette's, soft. "But we really just wanted to meet you ahead of time, when we could talk without all the glitz and glamour that we figure tomorrow night will hold."

Legend nodded, glancing at Riley, who smiled and winked at her slightly, as if to say, *I told you so.*

"Georgette was our firstborn," Teresa said. "And we were so surprised when she joined the Marines, but we were also really proud of her."

Legend nodded. "She was a good Marine."

Teresa smiled.

"In her letter, she called you something different than Legend," George said. "Is Legend a stage name kind of thing?"

"No, sir. George—Georgette," she corrected, "probably referred to me as Ustura, which is my given name. It translates directly into Legend." She grinned. "Legend was easier for the Marines to pronounce."

"Ustura?" George repeated, stumbling over the pronunciation. "Am I saying that right?"

Legend smiled. "It's *oo*, like in *moo*."

"Ustura," George tried again.

"Much closer."

"And what nationality is that?" Teresa asked.

"It's Israeli."

"Is your family from Israel?" George asked.

"My father was, yes. They live up north now, in Oregon."

"I see," George said. "So how did you meet Georgette?"

"We were stationed at the same base. She came across me running my mad off."

"I'm sorry?" George looked confused.

"I tended to get myself in trouble with my mouth in the Marines," Legend said. "So whenever something would make me mad, I'd go to the track and run until I was too tired to say something I shouldn't. She was on the track one day when I was doing that."

"Oh," George said, nodding.

"She didn't like to see people unhappy," Teresa said. "She was forever befriending the people that other people avoided."

"Well, that explains why she befriended me," Legend said, grinning.

"Troublemaker, were ya?" George asked.

"I tended to be rather vocal about things I didn't like, which was a lot about the Marines and the way they treated women."

"I can see how that could be difficult," George said. "So, I wanted to ask you something," he continued. "But I'm not sure how to ask it exactly."

"Just ask, sir," Legend said.

"Was our daughter… Was she…"

"You want to know if she was a lesbian before she met me?"

"It's nothing against you," Teresa said, reaching out to touch Legend's hand, which rested on the table. "We just worry that we missed something."

"Like your daughter being a lesbian and not telling you?" Legend asked, gentling her voice on the last as she realized how it had sounded. "I'm sorry," she said, shaking her head. "That wasn't fair. The answer is no. At least, she didn't think she was when we met. We specifically had a conversation about it when she asked me if I was, and she said that she wasn't and wanted to know if we could still be friends."

George and Teresa exchanged a relieved look. "We were very religious people for a long period of time, and we worried that Georgette joined the Marines to get away from us because she couldn't tell us she was gay."

"Well, I think you're pretty safe on that score," Legend said, smiling sadly. "I think the gay was... well, my fault."

"Why do you think that?" George asked.

"I'm the one she decided to be gay with."

"But you can't help that she cared about you that much."

"She tried," Riley said, looking over at Legend.

"What does that mean?" George asked Riley.

Legend put her hand over Riley's as a way of silencing her. "She means that I tried to keep Georgette at arm's length."

"Bet that didn't work," George said. "Georgette always got what she wanted when she set her mind on something."

Legend laughed softly. "Well, that was definitely the Georgette I knew."

Suddenly she felt a lump in her throat. She did her best to force it away as the waitress came up to take their order.

"I, uh," Legend said, looking over at Riley. "Can you order for me? I'll be right back. Excuse me," she said to George and Teresa as she grabbed her jacket and walked away from the table.

Riley nodded, having seen the stricken look on Legend's face. She watched her stride out, already reaching for her cigarettes.

She ordered Legend a sandwich and beer, then food for herself. As George and Teresa ordered, Riley was looking out front and could see Legend smoking, her hand shaking slightly as she lifted the cigarette to her mouth.

"Is she alright?" Teresa asked.

Riley took a deep breath, blowing it out as she nodded. "You need to know that this has been really hard on her. She loved your daughter very much, and losing her was devastating for her. Even nine years later, she's still very affected."

George nodded. "You played our daughter in the movie, is that right?"

"Yes," Riley said. "Legend said I look a lot like her."

"You do," Teresa said, smiling.

"I'm going to tell you something that Legend isn't going to tell you, but I think you need to know it before you see that movie tomorrow night. Everything you see in that movie is what really happened. She was adamant about the way we made it, and made sure everything was a perfect recreation. She's paying homage to your daughter and what happened to her. The only thing she did change originally was the end—she made it so your daughter survived and was sent home to you. She's since changed that, because we felt that your daughter's tragic sacrifice was important and the whole truth needs to be told."

George and Teresa looked very surprised. "We thought it was going to be a very Hollywood version," George said.

"No, Legend wouldn't allow that. She made it gritty and true," Riley said, looking out to where Legend was pacing. "And something else you should know—and please don't ever tell her I told you this—Legend tried to take her own life after we wrapped the movie. She wanted to join your daughter."

"Oh…" Teresa said, tears in her eyes as she looked over at her husband. George looked very affected as well.

"This movie is extremely important to her," Riley said. "And you need to know that she poured everything she has into it so she could tell your daughter's story. It cost her a lot, emotionally and physically."

George and Teresa nodded, looking grave. Riley saw that Legend was headed back inside.

"One last thing," she said to George. "Ask her about the dog tag she wears."

Legend got back to the table as George nodded, his eyes going to the dog tag at Legend's neck.

"Sorry," Legend said as she sat back down, putting her jacket back on the chair.

Teresa reached out to touch her hand again. "Are you alright, dear?"

Legend smiled softly, looking at Teresa's hand as she nodded. "Things just get a little rough sometimes. It's kind of been that way during all of this."

"It seems like you really loved our daughter," George said.

"I did, sir, believe me."

"I do," he said, nodding, then canted his head at the tag. "That's an interesting version of a dog tag," he said. "Can I see it?"

Legend's expression flickered. She'd never taken it off since she'd put it on, on the one-year anniversary of Georgette's death. She took a deep breath and unclasped it, then handed it to George. He examined it, then turned it over, even as Teresa leaned over to look at it as well.

"G.T.G.," George said softly as he touched the letters.

Legend nodded, looking emotional again.

"This is for her?" George asked, glancing up at Legend.

"Yes, sir," she said. "I never got to see her again after I found her—they'd sent her home before I could... And I didn't know where..." She took a deep breath. "I didn't know where she was buried, so..."

"Well, we'll have to remedy that," George said, tears in his eyes as he handed Legend back the dog tag.

Legend nodded as she put it back on. Riley reached over and took her hand, squeezing it gently.

Their lunch arrived a short while after, and Legend accepted the beer gratefully. They talked about other things then, and at one point, George handed Legend an envelope.

She saw Georgette's handwriting on it and closed her eyes slowly, nodding. She reached back, sliding the letter into her pocket, knowing she couldn't read it in front of them, because she knew she was going to be a mess if she did.

After lunch they walked out to the front. George got a good look at Legend's car and talked to her about it while Teresa and Riley discussed what they were wearing for the premiere. As they parted ways, George took Legend into his arms, hugging her tightly.

"Thank you for making my daughter so happy," he said, tears in his voice. "I just wish you could have had a lifetime together."

Legend was crying when they parted.

Teresa hugged her as well, kissing her cheek. Riley hugged them both and said she'd see them at the premiere the next night.

Mom, Dad, I wanted to tell you that I met someone, and I'm completely and utterly in love! It's probably going to come as a surprise to you, but the person I'm in love with is a woman. What you need to know is that she's such an amazing person! She was my very first friend here, and she is the one that encouraged me to get into radio communications like I wanted to when I joined. She's an incredible videographer for the Marines, so talented! She's strong and beautiful and has the most amazing eyes I've ever seen, sometimes green and sometimes gold. And she loves me! Of course, because of Don't Ask, Don't Tell we have to be so careful. It's horrible! They watch everything she does because she is a lot more different-looking than me, and I think there is a lot of jealousy about her because she's a major and half of these guys can't even make second lewy! She's always telling me to be careful, and not to draw suspicion to myself. She tries to take care of me all the time. Just like you always did, Daddy, when I wanted to climb a tree or go swimming in the river. She's just like that! I love that she's protective of me, and I know that for her it would be awful for them to find out about her being gay, because they would run her right out of here. The last thing I want to do is ruin her career, so I do whatever she tells me to do to keep us safe. I hope one day you can meet her. She's an incredible person.

I have to go. I'm sorry if this is all very shocking, but I love you guys and I wanted to tell you that I've finally found love!

Your daughter, no matter what,

Love, Georgette

Legend felt sick. Tears streamed down her cheeks. She was sitting out on the back patio. Riley had left her alone to read the letter Georgette had sent to her parents years ago. It was dated six months before her death. It stabbed at Legend again that Georgette had been worried about ruining Legend's career, not her own. She sat out on the patio for a couple of hours that afternoon, but before long it was time to get dressed for the premiere.

Wearing a perfectly tailored suit of charcoal gray, with a crisp white shirt and black leather dress boots, Legend made the perfect edgy Hollywood director. With Riley on her arm wearing a black Armani dress that was cut to fit her perfect shape and expose the arms she'd worked so hard for, they made the hot Hollywood couple.

As everyone settled in their seats, Legend walked up to the podium.

"I need to say a few things before you see this film. First and foremost, I want to acknowledge Georgette Griffin's family," she said, gesturing toward the rows in front where Georgette's whole family sat. "You have no idea how happy I am that you are here," she said, smiling softly. "Of course, I want to thank the entire cast and crew. You know who you are." She grinned. "For putting up with my ass the entire time. There were a lot of changes, rearrangement, and drama…" She trailed off as she touched eyes with Talon and Riley. "Many of you may not know this, but this film is an incredibly accurate depiction of my life in my last year in the Marines, before I was discharged under Don't Ask, Don't Tell. Georgette Griffin was the woman I was with when this happened. This is her story as much as it is mine." She looked directly into Riley's eyes. "I've loved two women in my lifetime," she said seriously. "I lost the first one to Don't Ask, Don't Tell, and I found the second one during the making of this movie. I love you, Riley. Thank you for keeping me alive to make this movie and see it through."

There were a lot of shocked looks as Legend stepped away from the podium and went back to her seat. Then there was a roar of applause as everyone saw her lean over and kiss Riley softly, her hand at her cheek.

Two hours later, as the movie drew to a close, Riley was completely shocked when instead of Talon's voice on the voiceover, it was Legend's, with a clip of Legend lying in a bunk, like the one in the barracks, wearing the khaki tank top, her dog tags, and BDU pants and boots, her light eyes staring up at the camera unseeing.

"My name is Legend Azaria. This was my story and Georgette's. I lost the love of my life that day at the base. I never even got to say goodbye. As for me, I lost my commission, I lost my career, and at one point I almost gave up my life. Don't Ask, Don't Tell wasn't a safeguard for gays—it was a career killer, and it ruined lives. It's been estimated that at least 13,425 men and women were discharged under DADT. All those lives ruined, careers ruined, because of something that was no one's business. On September 20, 2011, Barack Obama repealed Don't Ask, Don't Tell, allowing gay men and lesbians to serve openly in the military for the first time ever. It was too late for Georgette and me, but it changed lives. This movie is dedicated to all those men and women who served their country under the cloud of DADT and did their jobs anyway. Thank you for your service."

As the credits rolled, every person in the theater gave a standing ovation. It took a half hour for people to start leaving. Legend was surrounded, so many people telling her how amazing the movie was; there were tears in a lot of eyes that night, including those of Georgette's family.

As the crowd started to disperse, Riley turned to Legend. "Did you tell me you love me for the first time in front of hundreds of people?"

"Just be happy I didn't ask you to marry me in front of them," Legend said, her light eyes sparkling.

Epilogue

For the Telling received critical acclaim and was hailed as the most incredibly honest work critics had seen in years. It was nominated for multiple Academy Awards, including best screenplay, best movie soundtrack, and best musical score, as well as for best actress, best supporting actress, and directing. It was also nominated for best picture. Legend was pleased, but what she liked more was that people were seeing the movie and saying that it changed their lives, or changed their views on gays in the military. What she liked was that people were now talking about things that they hadn't discussed in a while, or ever.

A month after the premiere, on the beach outside her Malibu home, Legend presented Riley with a 2.4-carat Martin Katz diamond engagement ring, even going down to one knee to propose. Riley gladly accepted. Legend was happier than she'd ever been. Finally, she'd found someone she was free to love, and who had seen her at her very worst and loved her anyway.

Georgette's family had stayed in touch, congratulating Legend not only on the Oscar nominations but on her engagement to Riley. They were shocked when she sent them regular royalty checks, having assigned 5% of the profits of *For the Telling* for Georgette's family shortly after being contacted by Georgette's father, before they'd ever even met. George Griffin had called Legend and told her that her generosity was appreciated but not necessary.

"Sorry, George," Legend said with a smile. "You're just going to have to figure out how to spend that money. Take Teresa on a cruise, send the grandkids to college... buy a retirement home."

Two months later, the group made a road trip to Vegas for Legend and Riley's wedding. Classic cars, new cars, sports cars, muscle cars all caravanned the route. A number of races ensued; Memphis became the reigning champion, beating Quinn's Mach with her brand new Porsche GTR-3, by seconds.

They took over a bar called The Free Zone the night before the wedding, dancing, drinking, and causing general mayhem. At one point the bois were outside smoking, and the conversation got interesting.

"So, how many of your leading ladies did you get to?" Quinn asked Legend.

Legend's lips curled in a grin. "Uh..."

"All of 'em, is what I heard," Jet said, grinning wickedly.

"Nope," Legend said, shaking her head. "Didn't get to Allexxiss Ramsey-Sparks."

"Did you ever a have a shot there?" Rayden asked.

"I didn't even try. I like my head where it's at—I tend to think BJ Sparks would relocate it for me."

"Yeah, like somewhere in this desert," Remington said, laughing.

Legend nodded. "Yeah."

"So..." Skyler said. "Anyone else you didn't get to?"

"Technically, Riley was a supporting actress…"

"Ho!" Cody and Dakota said at the same time.

"Talon's not my type," Legend said, grinning.

"That one's hard to pin down," Jericho said. "She's a girl one minute, then she's one of the bois… It must be entertaining, trying to keep up with her. I feel sorry for the woman that lands that one."

Everyone chuckled at that.

"So, I'm hearing from Riley that a lot of you have some fairly interesting stories in your pasts and/or presents," Legend said, her eyes sparkling.

"Oh shit…" Lyric said, shaking her head. "Now we've done it—we've let a movie maker into the group. We're all gonna end up on the damned big screen."

"As long as Taylor Momsen plays me, I'm good," Harley said.

The group got a good laugh out of that, and then the discussion ensued as to who would want which actress to play them in the movie.

"You bois think you're funny, but I'm taking mental notes here," Legend said.

"I think Ellen Page should play Cody," Dakota said, grinning.

"She's a brunette, dumbass—she'd more likely play you," Cody replied.

Dakota laughed. "You never heard of bleach?"

"Now, let's talk the girls…" Memphis said.

"Oh yeah, that would get dangerous," Kai said, chuckling. "Hell, my girl could play herself—she's got the genes for it."

"No fair," Tyler said. "I'd want Elena Satine to play Shen."

"Who the hell is that?" Jet asked.

"She's a Russian actress, and hotter than hell," Legend said, her eyes sparkling.

"Oh yeah," Tyler said, grinning.

"What was she in?" Skyler asked.

"*Magic City*—it was a series, short-lived, but she's a good actress," Legend said. "Maybe we need to talk, Ty…"

"Uh-oh," Tyler said, rolling her eyes.

"Hey, you and Shen's story is right in line with what Legend did with *For the Telling*," Skyler pointed out.

"Is it now…" Legend said, looking more interested.

"Yeah, they were a classic DADT story, and Shen was straight too, wasn't she?" Jet said.

"Shut up, Jet," Tyler said, her eyes narrowed.

"Really?" Legend asked. "Shenin was straight when you met her? You two are Air Force, aren't you?"

"Yes, and we still are," Tyler said. "And I had to hold Shen off till DADT was repealed, actually, because like you, I didn't want to ruin either of our careers or lives."

Legend nodded. "Oh, yeah, we need to talk."

"Shen's gonna kill me…" Tyler said, shaking her head.

Jet and Skyler both grinned.

"You two need to just shut the hell up, or I'll start talking about your stories. In fact, Legend, did you know that Jet went back to Iraq to rescue her wife out of the clutches of ISIS?"

Legend glanced at Jet, her eyes widening with interest. "Really..." she said, her voice trailing off as her eyes sparkled again.

"I hate you, Ty..." Jet said, narrowing her eyes at her.

Tyler only chuckled. "You started it."

"Yeah, I can see some long conversations here," Legend said, finishing her cigarette. "In the meantime, though, I need about ten shots and to dance with my soon-to-be wife."

Everyone agreed to that readily enough. It was a fun evening.

The wedding between Legend Azaria and Riley Taylor was held at the Aria hotel, in The Gallery, which featured Dale Chihuly glass artwork. It was an intimate setting, with the guests surrounded by such incredible pieces. When Riley had found the place, she'd known it was something perfect for her and Legend; it was the kind of dramatic, colorful art that Legend favored and which Riley had come to love as well.

Legend wore a tuxedo with slim-fitting pants, with two-inch-heeled black suede boots, a crisp white shirt with a banded collar, and a fitted jacket with thin satin lapels that fell to her mid-thigh and cut in sharply at her waist. She stood alone at the end of the aisle, waiting for Riley.

Riley wore a blush-colored Pnina Tornai strapless mermaid-style gown that was fitted to her knees and then flared, with jeweled appliques that served to emphasize her small waist and perfect body. Her long hair was pulled up, with curls hanging down attractively in a few places. She looked incredibly beautiful.

The song "Permission" by Sixx:A.M. played while she walked

down the aisle. Legend had gotten her "okay" on the song, because it was part of *The Heroin Diaries*; it was a ballad that seemed to really fit them. The lyrics talked about removing the emotional armor she'd built up over the years and trying to make amends for all she'd done. Most poignant, however, was the line "your permission is all I need to heal."

When Riley reached Legend, Legend took her hand.

"You look absolutely incredible," Legend whispered.

"You look pretty fantastic yourself," Riley said, winking.

The ceremony was short and sweet. They'd removed all references to God, or any kind of nonsense about obeying anyone, because there was no way that was ever happening with either of them. Legend added a band of diamonds to the engagement ring she'd given to Riley; Riley slid a platinum band etched with the Hebrew symbols for love and trust onto Legend's left ring finger. Legend gazed at the ring, turning it to see the symbols, then looked up at Riley.

"How?" she asked.

Riley smiled. "I asked someone."

"Amazing, thank you."

When the officiant pronounced them married and said that Legend may kiss her bride, she stepped in, putting her hand to Riley's cheek, kissing her gently at first, and then deepening the kiss as Riley grasped her shoulders, moaning softly.

The catcalls started immediately as everyone clapped and cheered.

It was an auspicious beginning to a happy life.

Follow the author and find out more about her series here:

Website: www.sherrylhancock.com

Facebook: @SherrylDHancock

Twitter: @Sherryl_Hancock

Also by Sherryl D. Hancock:

The *MidKnight Blue* series. Dive into the world of Midnight Chevalier and as we follow her transformation from gang leader to cop from the very beginning.

www.vulpine-press.com/midknight-blue-series

The *Wild Irish Silence* series. Escape into the world of BJ Sparks and discover how he went from the small-town boy to the world-famous rock star.

www.vulpine-press.com/wild-irish-silence-series

Lightning Source UK Ltd.
Milton Keynes UK
UKHW040722160320
360408UK00001B/74